To Nic

IMPOSSIBLE

TALES!

Eight extraordinary stories which will blow your mind

Chase your dreams and
always believe that
anything is possible!

D. Worsley

DAN WORSLEY

For Mum and Dad

<u>CONTENTS</u>

CHEWED UP

Most people are afraid of something. It is a fact of life and something we all just have to accept and try to face up to. There are some folk who turn to jelly at the sight of a scuttling spider or a slithering snake. Others turn into a quivering wreck when faced with having to swim, or look down from a tall building.

I class myself differently to those people, as my phobia is very unusual and one which you will probably laugh at and will never have heard of before. You see, I could jump from a plane and skydive, or hold a venomous snake without even breaking a sweat. But if you told me I had to face a pair of false teeth, I think I would collapse onto the ground in a traumatised mess. You see, I'm the only person in the world to suffer from this horrible condition, which my doctor has labelled 'Chomperphobia'.

Over the years, I have had many different treatments and I am just about coming to terms with my dreadful condition. I haven't always been this way though, and I completely blame my current situation on a series of events which happened many years ago.

It all began during a weekend away at Gran's farm. Mum and Dad had plans that weekend and it was decided that I was to be packed off to stay with Gran. This happened regularly and things usually went without a hitch. This visit was to turn out very differently.

As we pulled up at the padlocked gate on the road to the ramshackle, old farmhouse, I cast my eyes across the never-ending cornfields which stretched as far as I could see.

Huge barns and buildings were dotted around the central farmhouse, from which Gran emerged, waving frantically and striding down the dusty track to let us through the farmhouse gate. Wearing green wellies, a blue pair of dungarees and a checked shirt, she looked as she always had; her clothes remained the same as I had always remembered.

Unlocking the gate and swinging it open, she waved us through and followed the car up the track. Leaning in through the open passenger window, she placed a slobbery kiss on my cheek. "Well hello," said Gran as her wild, black hair blew in the breeze.

"Thanks for having Erin for the weekend," replied Mum, as I clambered out and removed my bag from the boot.

Placing a suntanned arm around me, Gran hugged me tightly and we waved as Mum turned the car around and headed off down the dirt track.

"Come on, let's get in," instructed Gran as she gazed up to the sky. "Looking at those clouds, it looks like there is a storm on the way."

As I looked up, I could see threatening, black clouds which were rolling in. A cool breeze had begun to create waves through the corn, which stood like rows of soldiers in the fields.

Following Gran as she opened the front door, I dumped my bag on the floor and flopped down in the armchair in the corner of the room. The long journey had taken it out of me and I was absolutely shattered.

As I looked around the lounge I realised nothing had changed over the years I had been visiting. Gran had been frozen in time since Gramps had died just over eight years ago. Leaving things as they were seemed her way of clinging on to life before Gramps had passed away.

"I am guessing you're starving," Gran said handing me a glass of water. "Well don't worry, because I have a slap-up meal ready for you," she said with a huge grin. Mouth-watering smells wafted into the lounge. I salivated in anticipation of the feast which was to come.

"Lovely, thanks. I'm ravenous," I replied before gulping down the water and further savouring the glorious smells which had now entirely filled the lounge.

Gran disappeared back into the kitchen, and before long we were sitting at the table tucking in. Gran carved a whole chicken and placed the succulent cuts of meat on my plate. I added several dollops of creamy mashed potato and assorted vegetables before flooding my plate with thick gravy.

As I tucked into the delicious dinner, I noticed Gran was sitting with her arms folded and was not eating. "Not hungry tonight?" I asked, wondering how I was going to get through the belly-busting banquet on my own.

"Unfortunately, it isn't my lack of appetite," she said as she rubbed the side of her face. Slipping her fingers into her mouth, she pulled out a saliva-coated set of false teeth. Holding them in the palm of her hand, she inspected them carefully, like a jeweller checking out a valuable diamond. "I only had them made last week, but something isn't right. They feel really uncomfortable."

Gran's explanation was rudely interrupted as the world outside seemed to explode and our conversation was stopped dead. A neon flash of lightning lit up the room and a huge thunderclap noisily boomed and shook the farmhouse. The lights flickered and temporarily dimmed before gradually glowing back to full brightness.

Gran placed the teeth on the table before standing up and making her way over to the window. Stopping eating and placing my knife and fork on the table, I followed her over to watch the incredible electrical storm, which was now taking place just as Gran had predicted a short while earlier.

Without warning, the sky brightly lit up again and the farmhouse shook violently. We were both thrown to the floor and the building was plunged into total darkness. Trying to stay calm, I called out to Gran.

She grabbed my arm and calmly spoke. "Are you alright, Erin? Looks like the farmhouse generator has taken a direct hit from that bolt of lightning. It must have blown the electrics. You stay here and I'll go and get a torch from the kitchen."

As my eyes adjusted to the pitch-black darkness, I could just about make out Gran's silhouette as she cautiously fumbled her way across the lounge.

Outside, torrential rain battered on the tin roof like bullets being sprayed from a machine gun. Thunderclaps boomed and rumbled overhead, causing the house to shake to its foundations. The storm was intensifying and the gentle breeze had transformed into a brutal wind which was repeatedly charging at the farmhouse, seeking out any weaknesses it could exploit.

Suddenly, my ears picked out a different type of noise

above the storm which raged outside. Trying to filter out the new noise from everything that was going on around me, I located the source of the strange clacking noise which seemed to be coming from the dining table.

Sitting still in the darkness, I listened intently to the bizarre click-clacking which seemed to be getting louder and nearer to me. My eyes scanned the room, but the pitch darkness prevented me from picking out the source of the noise.

Suddenly, a beam of light appeared from the direction of the kitchen and shone directly into my eyes, causing me to shield my face. "What's that strange noise?" asked Gran as she moved the torch around, sending the light beam darting in all directions before it finally settled at the table. "Where are my teeth?" Gran called out in a confused voice.

Before I could answer, my eyes detected movement on the wooden floor. The clacking noise grew louder and appeared to be getting closer. "They are over here, and they are alive!" I wailed as a lightning bolt temporarily lit up the room, to reveal Gran's gnashers in all their horrific glory as they rattled their way across the wooden floorboards. The devilish dentures were opening and closing at high speed as they clanked and clacked their way towards me. The plastic teeth were alive!

Gran redirected the light beam in the direction of the noise and the terrifying teeth were highlighted for us both to see. "They're coming for me!" I yelled as I picked my feet up and placed them on the chair I was perched on.

Suddenly, the chair began to vibrate and shake. Gran moved the beam again to illuminate the chair leg. Hearing a sound similar to a chainsaw cutting a tree down, I clung on to the arms of the chair as the vibrations rattled through my body.

The chair suddenly began to tip as its wooden leg gave way and I was sent sprawling onto the floor. The clacking noise began to change direction and was now heading directly towards me. Gran frantically searched the floor with the torch beam to find the chattering chompers, so that I could see exactly where they were.

Clambering to my feet, I tried to make sense of what was going on. I was being hunted down by a pair of plastic teeth. Surely this couldn't be happening. Could it?

"The lightning strike must have brought the little rascals to life," yelled Gran. "Head towards the torch light," she called as I followed the blinding beam.

Behind me, the clacking noise had intensified and the teeth were now chattering and clacking at a higher speed. The deadly dentures were picking up the pace in their pursuit of me!

Finally, I reached the source of the light and was dragged into the kitchen by Gran, who promptly slammed the door shut. Wedging a chair under the door handle, we both huddled on the floor at the far end of the kitchen. We listened. We waited. The storm still raged outside but at that moment in time, it was the least of our concerns.

Suddenly, the temporary calm was shattered as the kitchen door began to noisily rattle and shake. Gran fixed the torch beam on the bottom of the door and before our eyes, the wood began to splinter and crack.

"They're eating their way through the door," I wailed as

Gran grabbed my arm and hauled me to my feet. As we stood up the lower part of the door burst open and the terrifying teeth made their way through the hole which they had chewed in the door.

Darting across the kitchen, Gran grabbed the mop which was standing in a bucket in the corner of the room. Taking the torch from her, I searched the floor for the nasty gnashers before I spotlighted them in the beam.

Stepping forward with the metal shaft of the mop pointed out in front of her, Gran jabbed and prodded at the teeth like a zookeeper trying to control a wild beast. She did all she could to halt the murderous charge of the marauding molars, but ultimately her efforts proved ineffective. What happened next was totally beyond belief!

The terrible teeth clamped onto the end of the mop and began to gobble it up! Shards of metal flew up into the air as the mop handle shortened with every bite. Within seconds the mop was half of its original size as the teeth made light work of the metal shaft. Launching the remains of the mop across the room, with the chewing chompers still attached, Gran and I burst out of the back door and into the pouring rain.

"Head for the truck!" Gran yelled. She could barely be heard over the raging storm which still rumbled overhead.

Yanking open the door, I jumped into the passenger seat as Gran slid into the driver's seat beside me. We both closed the doors and Gran frantically searched for the spare set of keys. She pulled down the sun visor and searched through the glove box. No joy! All the time she was searching, I could see the bloodthirsty teeth making their way across the grass as they headed towards us like a missile locked on to a target.

"Right, we are going to have to make a run for it," Gran urged. "We'll head for the barn, then we can get up in the hayloft where we will be safe."

Just as I was about to answer, the car violently rocked and jolted before it began to shake from side to side. Looking in the wing mirror, I could see the teeth clamped onto the back tyre. They were chewing and chomping at the rubber in an attempt to halt our escape. A loud bang signalled they had been successful, as the tyre exploded and the car leaned over to one side.

Gran pushed her door open and made a break for it which left me with little option. Swinging the passenger door open, I stepped out onto the saturated grass and turned to run towards the barn.

Before I could take a stride, I felt a vice-like grip on my left foot. To my horror, I saw the troublesome teeth clamped onto the toe of my left trainer. Letting out a terrified howl, I began to tear at the laces before yanking my foot out and throwing the trainer across the farmyard. Unbelievably, the teeth continued to gobble up the remains of my trainer before they headed towards me in their relentless pursuit.

Running and splashing my way through the puddles, I darted through the gloom in the direction of the barn. Turning to look over my shoulder, I saw the cruel chompers emerge from behind the car and begin to head in my direction. Looking back to see where I was going, I was too late to spot an old barrel lying in my path.

Flying head over heels into the air like a launched rocket, I landed in a muddy puddle and instantly felt a searing pain shooting up my left shin. I tried to stand on my injured limb, but my leg could not take my weight and I instantly fell back down.

Clutching my leg, I looked over the barrel to check on the progress of the teeth. They were weaving their way nearer and nearer. They were clacking and chattering as if they were laughing at my dire predicament. Crawling on my belly and dragging my body along, I tried to escape, but the murderous molars were gaining on me at an incredible rate. I realised that my time was up and I was done for!

All of a sudden, the barn doors erupted in an explosion of splintering wood and blinding lights. The deafening revving of an engine signalled the arrival of my saviour as Gran hurtled out at high speed, sitting in the cab of her combine harvester. She pumped her fist in the air and blew the horn as she powered the machine into the farmyard. Menacing, mechanical blades were whirring and gnashing at high speed as she turned the huge vehicle and stepped on the throttle to send it powering in my direction. It looked like this was the end, but what a horrifying choice I was left with! I could either be eaten alive by a pair of possessed, plastic teeth or get sliced into strips by the razor-sharp blades of the advancing combine harvester.

Closing my eyes, tensing my body and curling into a tight ball, I prepared myself for my fate. Above the roar of the engine, I suddenly heard a grinding noise and I peeked between my fingers to see tiny shreds of plastic spraying high up into the air from the hungry blades of the machine, before showering back down onto the waterlogged farmyard floor. Gran had done it. She had chopped up the chompers!

"We got them," yelled Gran as she brought the machine to a halt, killed the engine and began to clamber down the ladder from the cab. "I totally shredded them up!" Gran hollered as she danced a victory jig through the puddles.

Helping me to my feet, Gran hugged me tightly before inspecting my wounded leg. "Think we need to get that looked at," she said as blood soaked through my trouser leg and an intense pain crept up into my knee.

I hobbled towards the farmhouse as the torrential rain still cascaded down and the storm raged all around us. Gran placed a sloppy kiss on my forehead and flashed me a gummy grin. "Think I might try and manage without any false teeth from now on," she giggled. "They seem to be more trouble than they are worth!"

SUPERPOWER STEW

I don't know about you, but I absolutely hate Mondays. It's the worst day of the week by a million miles. The weekend is a distant memory and there are five full days of school to face. Five days which are guaranteed to be filled with boredom and supreme torture!

Now don't get me wrong, I don't hate school, but it just gets in the way of all of the fun stuff in life, like hiding spiders in my sister's lunch box or terrifying my neighbours while wearing my werewolf mask. Life is one big laugh to me, but little did I realise that my next joke would set in action a chain of events which would make this particular Monday one which I would never forget.

The day started in the usual way, with the children in my class milling about, chatting and laughing as we waited for Mr Rogers to arrive and the lesson to begin. Memories of the weekend were being shared and general chitchat echoed around the walls of the room as we made the most of a teacher-free moment.

Suddenly the door handle lowered and the wooden door shot open, which sent the class scuttling to their places like woodlice hiding from the sunlight. Silence ruled the classroom and all eyes were fixed on Mr Rogers as he strutted across to his desk, let out a heavy sigh and put down a huge pile of books. He scanned the room like a hawk, looking for the slightest opportunity to hand out a detention. Not a peep could be heard; you could have heard a pin drop. We all knew what was going to happen soon, though, and the tension was unbearable.

Pulling out his chair, he cast his eyes across the classroom once more, before slowly lowering himself down onto the seat. The moment of glory was nearly upon us!

What happened next was magical. It was a marvellously mischievous moment. As Mr Rogers's backside hit the seat, the loudest trumping noise erupted from behind the bewildered teacher, causing a hysterical wave of laughter to sweep the room. Children held their sides as their bodies jerked uncontrollably with fits of laughter. The rip-roaring backside explosion had caused chaos and some children pretended to waft away invisible smells while others mockingly held their noses and battled for their breath. It was absolute carnage and I was proud to say that every bit of it was my doing.

As fast as the mayhem had begun, it was over, as a clearly embarrassed Mr Rogers slammed a metal ruler down on his desk. Silence reigned again. Slowly standing up from his seat, he reached behind and lifted up a deflated, red whoopee cushion. Holding it aloft, he scanned the room. His face began to turn bright red, as if it was being filled with cherryade from chin to forehead. The rage inside him was building and at this point, I realised that this joke may have gone too far this time.

"Stewart Simmons!" Mr Rogers roared, staring me full in the face. "Is this your doing?"

Considering my options, I remembered what my parents had always told me; that honesty was the best policy. "Yes Sir," I uttered. "I thought it would be a bit of a laugh to brighten a dull Monday morning."

He began to shake with anger and uncontrollable fury.

"A bit of a laugh? You thought it would be funny, did you? Well, I hope you find serving detention every day for the next month a bit of a laugh too!"

The rest of the lesson was spent working in complete silence as we copied notes from an ancient textbook. The bell signalled escape for the rest of the class, but I remained behind, working in silence. Mr Rogers sat at the front of the class eating his lunch, regularly glancing at the clock and occasionally tutting, until he was happy that I had served my time for that day. With five minutes of lunch break remaining, I was released and proceeded to charge down the corridor towards the lunch hall to try and grab something to fill my rumbling belly.

As I raced into the virtually empty hall, I saw Mary the cook packing away and starting to wash up. My stomach growled out an unhappy complaint, which urged me to find food as quickly as possible.

Moving over to the kitchen area, I approached Mary, who turned around from the sink where she was washing up and gave me a friendly smile.

"Oh, Stewart Simmons, you have missed lunch. You must be starving. Where have you been?" she asked as she wiped her hands with a towel. "I haven't got much left apart from my own lunch," she explained, picking up a clear plastic tub filled with what I can only describe as blue sludge. "Take it," she said kindly, pushing the tub in my direction, "I'll eat something when I get home."

"Wow, thanks Mary," I weakly replied, taking the tub and inspecting it further. Noticing black blobs mixed into the blue gunk, I was naturally keen to get more details about the contents. "What exactly is it?" I asked.

"Oh I'm afraid I can't give you details, as it's my Mum's special stew," she whispered. "That recipe has been passed on through my family, but it is a secret."

Everyone knew that Mary was a little strange and this only confirmed it. She had worked in the school for many years and it seemed age was catching her up and affecting her mind.

Regardless of Mary's state of mind, I was absolutely starving and as revolting as the food looked, I didn't see that I had any other options. Pulling the lid off, I dug in my fork and scooped out a dollop of the blue stew and placed it in my mouth. Surprisingly, it tasted okay and was not half as bad as it looked.

"Get it down you, it will do you good," Mary urged as I tucked into the colourful cuisine. Before I knew it, I had devoured half of the contents of the tub and my hunger had been satisfied. As I tried to hand the tub back to Mary, she waved her hand at me and told me to keep the rest for later.

Placing the tub into my bag, I threw my arms around Mary and hugged her tightly to show my appreciation. To my amazement, she was not the frail, old lady I expected her to be. Her little body bulged and rippled with muscles and as she hugged me back I thought she would break my ribs with her powerful clench.

Pulling away from her, I looked her in the face. "Got to eat healthily," she said with a wink and a grin. "Think it's my stew that keeps me in good shape! I eat a bowl every day without fail."

After thanking Mary again, I headed out of the kitchen

and sprinted through school to the PE block. Straight away I noticed how my legs effortlessly carried me along. My legs tingled and the muscles bulged as I changed into my sports kit before heading out onto the field to join my classmates.

"Simmons! Simmons!" boomed a foghorn-like voice. Mr Bashworth, the PE teacher, waved desperately at me. "Come on lad. Shape yourself. It's your race and you're holding everything up."

Jogging down the field, my head felt light and the tingling in my legs intensified. By the time I took my place on the start line with the other boys, my legs felt like they were about to explode.

"How you have made it to this final, I will never know," mocked Matt Roberts, in the lane next to me. "I reckon you will do well to finish last," he added.

I didn't reply. It was taking all my effort to deal with the tingling, which had now crept to my upper body. I began to panic and raised my hand to get the teacher's attention. At that same moment, the starting gun fired. It was too late, I had to run!

And run I did! I sprinted like never before. My legs whirred and powered me at a speed which I had never experienced. Usually, I was the kid who plodded along and finished somewhere near the back, but today I surged ahead of the others. My leg muscles pumped and pulsed, powering me at breakneck speed. As I glanced sideways my eyes were met by the sight of empty lanes. Looking over my shoulder, I could see the other boys were a long way back down the track.

Holding my arms high above my head, I crossed the

finish line to see Mr Bashworth staring at me with his mouth gaping open and head shaking from side to side. "Crikey, Simmons! You have gone and broken the school sprint record. Have you been doing some extra practice? I have never seen anything like that during my twenty-six years of teaching!"

Smiling at him, I turned and headed back to sit with my class, who were cheering and clapping my turbo-powered performance. Sitting on the grass next to my best friend Tariq, I lay down and tried to take in what had just happened.

"How did you pull that off?" asked Tariq excitedly.

"Not sure," I replied. "Guess all my practice paid off. Plus I got a bit lucky," I said in an attempt to play down my victory.

"Well we will see how lucky you are in a few minutes. It's the discus next up and Max Commons looks unbeatable. That lad is superhuman and you'll need more than a bit of luck to beat him," said Tariq.

By this point, I had stopped listening and was focusing my attention on the twitching muscles and burning flesh which now had gone beyond a tingle and made me feel like my whole body was on fire.

Dragging myself to my feet, I headed over to my next event. Mr Bashworth explained the rules and wished us well, before calling Max Commons up to take his first throw. We all watched as he twisted his muscular body and launched the discus, which sailed high into the air before crashing onto the school field. This was met by a ripple of applause and Commons waved to the crowd and smugly grinned like a man who thought he had the win in the bag.

After watching the other boys take their turn, it finally got round to me. Picking the discus up in one hand, I slowly began to twist and spin. The muscles in my arms felt huge and they were visibly bulging out from under my T-shirt.

Releasing the discus, I watched as it sailed high up into the sky, passing the point at which Commons's throw had been recorded. But it kept going higher and higher. The officials with the measuring tape began to run backwards for cover as the discus headed towards them! Eventually it thudded into the turf at the far end of the field, beyond the marked out area.

I turned around, to be met by a stunned silence from the rest of the school. Mouths hung open and fingers pointed. Some children had even been recording my colossal throw on their mobile phones. "Guess I don't know my own strength," I said with a chuckle.

Well, the buzz back in the changing rooms was incredible. Everyone wanted to talk to me and the attention made me feel like a famous celebrity or an Olympic hero. It was an amazing feeling! For once, all the attention was on me for the right reasons and it felt fantastic.

As we walked home, Tariq and I stopped off at Bond's Coffee Shop for a milkshake. Dumping our bags, we ordered and sat ourselves down at a table by the window. "If I tell you something, would you promise to keep it a secret?" I asked. Tariq nodded at me as the waitress arrived with our shakes. As he slurped his drink, I told him all about Mary's stew and the strange sensations of super strength and speed I had encountered that afternoon.

Stopping slurping, Tariq sat up and looked me in the eye.

"So, you are telling me that what happened this afternoon was all down to Mary's stew? I think you are going bonkers if you want my honest opinion," he said, returning his mouth to the straw to drain the remains of his milkshake from the glass.

Leaning closer to Tariq, I lifted the box Mary had given me onto the table. "This stuff is super stew," I said, pushing the plastic tub across the table. "It gave me more strength and power than I have ever experienced."

"Well if that's true, then you're Super Stew just like Superman," Tariq said as he pushed away his empty glass and burst into fits of giggles.

Before I could say anything, Tariq's squeals of amusement were drowned out by high-pitched screams and yells from the street outside. Through the window, I saw people on the street scattering in all directions. Up the high street, at the top of the hill, I spotted a school bus weaving and snaking its way down the road. The vehicle was clearly out of control and dangerously lurched one way then the other. The terrified pedestrians were running for their lives. Other vehicles pulled off the road to avoid the runaway bus, which was gathering speed by the second.

Without thinking, I peeled off the lid of the plastic tub and poured the contents into my mouth. I frantically swallowed and gulped as I guzzled down the blue mixture. The cold mixture slid down my throat and made me gag and choke. Forcing myself to keep it down, I pushed the chair out from behind me and sprinted through the shop door and onto the chaos-filled street.

Running up the pavement in the direction of the bus, I

could hear the screams of the terrified children on board. The bus was now nearly level with me and I spotted the doors were wide open. My heart pounded and my legs powered me along at an incredible speed. Shops whizzed by in a blur. Mary's stew had definitely kicked in and I was feeling the full super effects!

Timing my move carefully and checking both ways for traffic, I bolted from the pavement and across the empty road towards the bus. The vehicle lurched menacingly towards me, causing me to throw myself forward into the air. My feet left the tarmac and I sailed gracefully through the air before landing on the metal steps of the bus.

Grabbing the hand rail, I hauled myself up, to see the driver slumped over the steering wheel. My ears were filled with the deafening screams and shouts of petrified children who clearly feared for their lives. I had to stop the bus, and I had to stop it now!

Placing both hands around the handbrake, I summoned up every ounce of strength I possessed. Yanking the lever upwards and pushing the brake pedal with my feet, I felt the bus begin to skid and slide on the tarmac road. The vehicle was gradually slowing and I kept it in a straight line by heaving the driver's limp body clear of the steering wheel and taking control of the vehicle.

As I looked out of the windscreen, my heart felt like it had temporarily stopped. There was a pedestrian scurrying across the road only a short distance ahead of the sliding bus. It was clear she would not make it across in time. A sickening thud of metal on bone signalled she had not made it as the bus collided with the helpless woman. My heart sank and I felt sick to my stomach.

When the bus finally ground to a halt, I leapt from the vehicle and looked back to see a crowd gathering in the road around the injured woman. As I got closer I could see her face, and my legs buckled underneath me. It was Mary! The stricken woman lay motionless in the middle of the road. I dropped to my knees and tears flowed down my cheeks.

Apart from being bundled into an ambulance and being asked lots of questions by the police, what happened afterwards is all a bit hazy. The next thing I clearly remember is Mum and Dad walking into the hospital waiting room and sweeping me up in a tidal wave of tears and hugs.

"Thank goodness you are safe," Mum said as she stroked my hair. "What were you thinking though, Stewart? You could have so easily been killed!"

"Don't be too harsh on him," added Dad. "Our Stewart saved all those kids on that bus. From what the police have said, even though what he did was incredibly dangerous and pretty daft, he acted like a real life superhero. We should be proud of him for once!"

As we talked, a doctor approached. "Are you all friends of Mary O'Grady?" he asked. We confirmed we were and followed the doctor down the corridor.

"Is she dead?" I suddenly blurted out, causing the doctor to stop in his tracks and turn around.

With a smile on his face, he pushed open the door of the room next to him. There, lying in a hospital bed, was Mary. "Stewart Simmons, my hero!" Mary exclaimed as a huge smile broke out on her face and she waved us over. Dashing to her and throwing my arms around her, I kissed her on the cheek before turning to see my parents and the doctor standing behind me.

"Miss O'Grady is a very lucky lady," explained the doctor. "To say she was hit by a bus, she has hardly any physical injuries apart from a couple of bumps and bruises. It seems that a combination of you slowing it down and Mary being so incredibly fit has saved her life. She has muscles like nothing we have ever seen and her bone strength is incredible, especially as she is seventy-four! The test results we gathered are the best I have ever seen in all my years working as a doctor." Smiling at us all and nodding, the doctor turned and left.

"Told you I ate a healthy diet," Mary said with a grin on her face. "A bowl of my stew a day keeps me in good shape!"

Mary beckoned me closer and began to whisper in my ear. "I think you deserve this," she said as she leaned over and pulled a tatty scrap of paper from her coat pocket which was lying on the chair at the side of the bed.

Carefully unfolding the paper, I read the hand-written line at the top of the sheet, which said 'O'Grady's Super Stew' and was followed by a list of ingredients and instructions. Mary had gifted me the secret recipe as a reward for saving her life! I excitedly pushed the paper into my pocket. Something told me that today wouldn't be the last time I would be sampling Mary's Superpower Stew.

BLOWN AWAY

Excited children crowded around, buzzing and swarming like bees around a hive. The fuss seemed to be caused by a large, blue poster which was plastered across the wall, just to the side of the main gates to school.

Jostling for position using my elbows, I battled my way through the gathered masses and eventually gained a position where I could read the information on the poster. In large black print, it read 'Smith Town Raft Race' and was followed by dates and further details in a smaller font, which I was unable to read due to the sea of children surging one way and the other.

Battling my way out and grateful for some space and air, I heard a familiar voice. "I reckon we could win that," chirped Zac, my best mate, as he danced from one foot to the other. "Each team needs two children, so I reckon you and I would stand a great chance. My Dad has lots of stuff we could use to build a raft."

Before I had a chance to answer him, the crowd parted as if by magic and the excited chatter died away to give rise to a hushed silence. I turned to see the huge figure of Butch Grimley striding across the grass toward the gathered crowd.

Butch scowled at the assembled mob before walking through the passageway of children to read the poster. Not far behind him was his sidekick and partner in bullying, Thommo Parry. Whatever these two said, you did. They told you to jump and you asked them how high. Nobody dared to mess with Butch and Thommo.

Turning to scan the crowd once more, Butch scraped back his long, greasy locks to reveal a solitary, twinkling diamond earring which reflected the afternoon sun. Thommo flashed a wicked grin, while alternating his attention from Butch to the crowd and back again. "Don't you little weasels get any ideas about winning this raft race," instructed Butch in a stern tone. "You might as well give up and not bother. There will only be one victorious pair, and that will be me and Thommo."

Nodding his head in agreement, Thommo's grin grew even wider, revealing a set of yellow teeth which clearly would have benefited from some quality time with a toothbrush. Moving back through the crowd, the pair headed off across the grass and disappeared around the school building.

"Well, it looks like that's that," Zac said in a disappointed tone.

"No!" I replied angrily. "Those two thugs aren't going to stop us taking part. There is £200 prize money up for grabs. Just think what we could do with that!"

"Okay, I'm in if you are," replied Zac, the smile slowly returning to his face.

Heading to class for the final session of the day, we settled down and waited for Miss Levante to begin the art lesson. Her thunderous expression signalled only one thing, this was going to be a tough end to the day! Slamming down a pile of books, she barked out her instructions to a hushed class who knew better than to do anything more than breathe if they valued their lives and their wellbeing.

It was at that moment that my day took a significant turn

for the worse. Between you and me, I have a bit of a 'problem' and as silence reigned and the class worked, my personal issue decided to rear its ugly head once again.

It all began with horrendous gurgling noises in my stomach, which growled and groaned like an angry bear. This was followed by some mild discomfort in my lower belly, which soon developed into sharp, stabbing pains and signalled to me that I needed to take immediate action.

Trying not to draw attention to my desperate plight, I rubbed my stomach in a vain attempt to ease the agony. It was no use though. Beads of sweat began to form on my forehead and panic and fear began to set in, which made the situation even worse.

Squirming in my seat and desperate to attract Miss Levante's attention, I raised my hand and silently pleaded that she would instantly spot me. She noticed me immediately, but her cruel streak meant that I would have to wait, as she started to shuffle paper on her desk to let me know that she would deal with me when she was good and ready.

After what seemed like minutes, but must have been merely seconds, she made eye contact. "Please could I nip to the toilet?" I anxiously requested, as I began to lift myself from my chair in anticipation of a positive answer.

Before she could reply one way or another, the silence of the classroom was shattered. My wicked bout of wind, which had been building in my belly, was finally unleashed for all to witness. The high speed explosion escaped like an express train leaving a tunnel. It vibrated on the plastic chair as it made its break for freedom and violently blew a pile of papers from the desk which was directly behind me, sending them high into the air.

Face as red as a post box, I half stood and half sat, feeling like a rabbit caught in headlights. Considering my next step, I glanced around the classroom as the papers fluttered down to the floor like seagulls falling from the sky. Some children were biting their lips as they desperately tried not to burst into fits of laugher, while others sat open-mouthed in shock at my backside's bad behaviour. Even Miss Levante's sour face had softened somewhat and she flashed a hint of a grin as she tried to regain her professional composure.

Before she could utter a word, I made a decision to make a break for it. Heading out of the stunned classroom, I burst into the deserted toilets and sat down in an empty cubicle. Reviewing the events of the previous few minutes in my head, I thought back over the years before. This had been a real issue for as long as I could remember and unfortunately it wasn't improving. In fact, as I grew older, the power and force of the windy explosions I suffered had grown in intensity.

Over the years, I had visited many different doctors, who had asked lots of questions and performed lots of tests. Unfortunately, none of them had been able to provide any answers or real solutions, apart from one who prescribed a special pill which I took each morning without fail. This had helped in some ways and, combined with a change in diet, had helped the situation. Despite this, there were still occasional eruptions like the one I had experienced in class and I just had to accept this was how it was going to be. My jet-powered trumps were just part and parcel of who I was.

As the school bell burst into life, signalling the end of the day, I heard the main toilet door open and noticed a pair of tatty trainers under the cubicle door which I instantly recognised. "Come on Jay," said Zac. "Let's go home. Worse things happen at sea. These things happen to us all."

Opening the cubicle door, I was pleased to see Zac's friendly smile and, grabbing my bag, we headed off.

Very few words were exchanged on the walk home that day, until we got to Zac's house. "Fancy making a start on the raft in the morning? Look at all the junk we could use," he added as he enthusiastically pointed at the barrels, wood and various other odds and ends which were scattered across the back garden.

Nodding in agreement I waved goodbye and took the short cut across the park. As I neared home, my heart sank as the terrible tummy twinges began once again. I began to half run, half scuttle in the hope that I could save myself from more public humiliation.

Pushing my key into the lock, I barged the door open and dived into the safe surroundings of home. Throwing my bag down in the hall, I rubbed my belly as I prepared for the forthcoming eruption.

At that same moment Hurricane, my pet cat, wandered out of the lounge to greet my arrival. Winding her body round my legs, she purred loudly and circled me before sitting down directly behind me. Giving me little warning, my latest tummy trauma was released. The powerful gust of wind hurtled out at a startling rate of knots and hit poor Hurricane full-on. The force of my bottom blast lifted the poor beast clean off the floor and sent her hurtling at high speed across the lounge, before she disappeared over the sofa.

"Oh Hurricane, I'm so sorry," I said as I dashed across the lounge to check on the cat's wellbeing before I discovered the poor animal crashed out on the floor.

Lowering myself down, I reached out to Hurricane and tried to give her an apologetic stroke. The traumatised beast hissed and spat, then lashed out with her claws outstretched! Jumping to her feet, she backed away in a state of confusion, before scampering away to seek a safe hiding place in the kitchen.

Getting to my feet, I felt tears prick my eyes. I dashed across the lounge and headed upstairs before I slumped face-down onto my bed and allowed the tears to flow into my pillow.

Firstly, I had been humiliated in front of my classmates, and to top the day off, I had sent the cat skywards and terrified the poor animal. Life was just not fair! I was sick of being different and constantly feeling like the odd one out. My intestinal incidents had turned me into a freak!

The next morning I was up and about before Mum had stirred. After gobbling down my breakfast and taking my medication, I grabbed my bike and headed round to Zac's house.

He was already in his garden and had made a start. As he was dragging a barrel across the lawn, he spotted me. "I reckon this raft will be as strong as the Titanic when we have finished," he said, causing me to smile and chuckle to myself.

"But the Titanic sank," I replied.

"Oh, you know what I mean," he said, as he began to tie a long piece of wood to the barrel.

After a morning of hard work and effort, we stepped back to inspect our creation. Four barrels were held together with long planks of wood which were lashed tightly together with rope. To strengthen the vessel even further, we had screwed the wooden planks together and bound them with tape which Zac found in his Dad's tool shed. Large sheets of wood formed the deck on top of the barrels, and a sail poked up from the middle of the deck which we had made from a sweeping brush and an old, white bed sheet. Two plastic chairs had been screwed to the deck, and by a stroke of luck Zac had found two old canoe paddles in the shed. "It looks awesome," squealed Zac in a voice which was bursting with excitement.

I smiled and nodded in agreement. "Let's just hope it floats," I said nervously. "I don't fancy swimming in Smith's river. The water looks a bit grim!"

"Oh don't worry," said Zac, brushing off my comment. "If it's a windy day tomorrow, I reckon we will get some extra speed up with that huge sail," he said tugging at the white bed sheet which gently flapped in the breeze.

It was at that precise moment an idea popped into my head. It was a cunning plan which could just help us to win the race. My Mum had always taught me to try and find solutions to my problems. Well, I realised that I had a big problem which could actually become a solution.

On my way home, I called into the local shop to purchase a few items which were a crucial part of my master plan. Placing the goods into my basket, I paid and headed home before creeping upstairs to stash the bag under my bed. I was aware that should Mum discover them, she would go bananas.

After heading downstairs, I sat at the table and waited for tea. Mum arrived within seconds and delivered a huge plate of steaming spaghetti. I was aware that this could pose a problem and could have put a spanner in the works of my plan. Half-heartedly, I ate a few forkfuls of the tomato drenched pasta, before pushing the remains around the plate.

"Not hungry tonight? Are you okay?" Mum asked in a concerned tone.

"I'm fine. I think it's nerves about the big race tomorrow," I replied, struggling to lie to Mum when she was genuinely worried about me. "I'm going to get an early night," I added, before heading through to the kitchen with my half-finished dinner. Placing the leftovers on the worktop, I checked the coast was clear before I carefully opened the drawer and took out the plastic tin opener. I slipped it into my pocket and headed upstairs.

Kneeling down on my bedroom floor, I reached under the bed and dragged out the carrier bag. I knew that I had to time my plan precisely and, looking at my watch, I realised it was crucial for stage one of the operation to take place. Reaching into the bag, I pulled out a food can. 'Mexican Chilli Beans' the label declared in bold, black text which was surrounded by orange and red flames. Removing the tin opener from my pocket, I began to open the can of beans, before finally lifting the lid completely off. I was good to go.

Raising the can up, I began to guzzle the contents. The chilli beans may have not been warmed up, but they were like an inferno in my mouth, and as they travelled down my throat the intense burning spread. Gulping and gasping, I managed to chomp the whole tin before placing the empty can back in the bag and letting out an enormous burp. Pushing the bag back under my bed, I lay down.

My mouth felt hot on a volcanic scale. Eating the fiery chilli beans had been like eating lava fresh from the volcano. My mouth, throat and stomach were on fire. I had to put up with it though, because it was all part of my plan.

After a couple of hours things began to settle a little bit, which told me it was time for stage two. Opening the remaining tin of beans, I performed the same routine of torture, which actually felt worse than the first. Gasping for air and wafting my burning lips, I chewed and swallowed until every last bean was gone.

Crashing onto my bed, I pulled up my T-shirt to reveal a bulging belly. It was time to get some rest before the excitement of the big race the next morning. Drifting off to sleep, I ran through my plan in my head and prayed things wouldn't backfire - literally!

I woke early with the sun creeping in through a gap in my blinds. The first thing I heard as I came to terms with the new day were the gargantuan groans and gurgles which were thundering from my bean-filled tummy. Pulling on my clothes, I popped my daily pill from the packet on my bedside table and swallowed it. It was important for my plan to work, but even I was not foolish enough to miss my daily medication.

Heading downstairs, I wolfed down a bowl of cereal and looked at my watch. The stomach grumblings had already begun and it was less than an hour to the race. Perfect. Things were going according to plan.

"Good luck," Mum shouted out of her bedroom window as I headed out onto the street on my bike. Waving to her, I headed down to Fiddlers Creek which would be the point where the rafts would all be launched. As I pedalled along, the grumbling in my guts grew and I knew that this was most definitely the calm before the storm!

As I approached the river, I heard excited chatter radiating from the children who were streaming towards the starting point. Vans with rafts inside them and cars towing trailers headed along the road which led down to Fiddlers Creek.

When I arrived, I could see at least twenty rafts waiting to be launched. I spotted Zac sitting on our creation, which was tied up on the riverbank. Heading over, he tossed me a life jacket which I put on along with a crash helmet. The helmet fitted perfectly, but it was a real struggle to get the life jacket fastened over my bloated belly. After a few adjustments, the fastener clicked and it was secure.

"Can't believe you bothered turning up," mocked a menacing voice from behind, which caused me to turn around immediately. There, stood in front of me, was Butch and his sniggering sidekick, Thommo. Looking at our raft, they both laughed like crazed hyenas before Butch pointed further up the bank. "That's a proper raft," he said as he waved his arm towards two red canoes which were taped together.

"You can't use those!" I bellowed. "That's cheating."

"It didn't say anything in the rules," he snarled, waving his fist at me. "Sure you won't want to complain to anyone will you?" he threatened, before turning and heading off with Thommo glued to his side.

"It's no good letting him wind you up," advised Zac. "We'll shut him up when we beat him."

The race organiser barked out instructions over a megaphone before he raised his starting pistol. The riverbank fell silent. That was apart from my stomach which was groaning and rumbling its angry message. The noises it was making were different to the usual racket it made and for a split second, I wondered if two tins of beans had been two tins too far.

Suddenly, the pistol loudly cracked and the silence turned to hysterical screaming and shouting. Zac and I heaved the raft forward and it slid down the wet bank and bobbed in the murky water.

"It floats!" yelled Zac as we both jumped aboard and began to paddle. Digging our paddles into the filthy water, the raft began to move forward and we slowly turned so that we were heading in the right direction.

As I looked back, Butch and Thommo were steaming towards us at high speed; the canoes cutting through the water like hot knives through butter.

As they approached a raft which was already wobbling from side to side, Butch reached out with his paddle and violently jabbed the unsteady craft, causing the girls on board to squeal and shriek. The crowd booed and jeered, but Butch and Thommo waved their paddles and cheered.

"You bullies!" I yelled as they moved past us. Butch gave me a look of hatred and slapped his paddle down hard against the water, sending a shower of filthy river water over me. Shaking with laughter, the terrible twosome headed off down the river.

Zac and I paddled with all our might, passing raft after raft and, most importantly, keeping Butch and Thommo firmly in our sights. The muscles in my arms burned and I gasped for air as my lungs felt like they would explode. As for my belly, it gurgled on and I knew that I couldn't hold our secret weapon back for much longer.

Looking across at Zac, I could see he was feeling the strain too. His face was screwed up and his teeth were gritted as he battled through the pain barrier to keep us moving. We were both determined to give it our best shot and if we were to lose, it would be in a blaze of glory.

As we navigated a bend in the river, Butch's canoe raft was still well ahead of us, but it was a gap we thought we could make up. Butch and Thommo may have been bullies, but they were extremely unfit bullies. They were both well out of shape and it was clear they were fast running out of steam. The gap between us was narrowing!

Miller's Bridge marked the finish line and it was quickly approaching. There was a gap of no more than 15 metres between the two rafts, but we were running out of river to catch them. Looking ahead, I could see Butch and Thommo waving and blowing kisses to the gathered audience. They thought the race was won, and were playing to the crowd.

My stomach was now swollen and ready to explode and

I couldn't hold back any longer. It was time for our secret weapon to be released. Throwing my paddle onto the deck, I carefully clambered to my feet on the rocking raft. Zac shot me a puzzled look, but he had no breath left with which to speak. Making my way to the rear of the raft, I turned my back to the sail and bent forward, placing my hands on my knees and aiming my bottom towards the bed sheet sail.

A torrent of powerful wind made its break for freedom, causing the sail to billow and flap wildly. The boat powered forward and moved at an incredible rate of knots, racing towards Butch and Thommo, who were still celebrating.

Hearing an ear-splitting groan rumbling from my grumbling guts, I repeated the windy feat yet again. The force was remarkable! This time I had to grab hold of a rope on the deck, as the blast was so extreme it nearly sent me tumbling into the murky water. The boat surged forward at an even greater speed and powered us past Butch and Thommo, who looked on with their mouths hanging open in shock and disbelief.

I watched as they grabbed their paddles and began to frantically splash, but it was all to no avail. They had lost. Our raft floated under Miller's Bridge, to be met by a chorus of cheering and clapping from the hundreds of spectators who had gathered. Zac and I punched the air in celebration of a remarkable win as we waited for our raft to drift to the bank.

As we were wearily clambering from the rickety raft onto the bank, I heard Butch's voice behind me. He was shouting and cursing and behaving like an angry snake trapped in a bag. What happened next was an accident; it was definitely not part of my plan.

The effort of clambering off the raft caused one last bean-powered explosion, which headed right towards Butch who was still jumping up and down on his raft in the middle of the river. By the time he had heard the eruption it was too late, and I turned to see him swept clean off his feet as the violent gust struck him in the chest and sent him crashing into the water. The crowd burst into fits of laughter as Butch splashed and wallowed like a drowning hippo in the filthy river.

Taking our arms and holding them aloft like victorious boxers, the man with the megaphone congratulated us and handed us our prize money. "I'm sure you will all join me in congratulating these two young raft racers on their fantastic victory," he said. "They've left us all completely blown away!"

JUNK FROM THE TRUNK

Loneliness had always been my best friend. Some people are blessed with many fantastic acquaintances and never-ending contact lists on their phones or social networking sites. Not me. I had never really been the popular type, but that never really bothered me or caused me to lose sleep. I didn't dwell on the fact or let it depress me. Please don't feel that I am in any way seeking your sympathy, or trying to make you feel so guilty that you will want to be a friend of mine. All I want to do is explain to you how my friendless existence, all those years ago, led me to one of the most incredible adventures you will ever hear about and changed my life forever.

Mr Jenks's Junkshop had been a regular fixture in our town and my life for as long as I could remember and was a place I regularly visited. When others were playing out together or having a kickabout on the park, I could usually be found in the little shop. It was sandwiched between a chip shop and a charity shop on a back street which most people never usually bothered venturing down.

Looking up at the weather-battered sign, it was clear that the shop had seen better days. The writing had long worn off and, combined with the filthy windows and paint peeling windowsills, made the place look tired and shabby and far from inviting. In fact, I liked it this way as it meant that most of the times I visited I was the only customer. This meant that I had more chance of unearthing that elusive piece of treasure which I had always hoped I would discover. If I was lucky, Mr Jenks would let me help out around the place, which I absolutely loved.

Pushing open the shop door, I heard the familiar tinkling of the brass bell which signalled to Mr Jenks he had a customer. You would imagine that most shop owners would show interest when there was the chance of a sale or a bit of business, but not Mr Jenks. He just sat at his desk at the far end of the shop and continued to scribble on a piece of paper which clearly was more important to him than his customers.

"Good morning," I called, awaiting a response from the shopkeeper.

The first part of Mr Jenks's response was pretty hard to make out, as it was more of a grunted growl than actual speech, and was worsened by the fact that his false teeth were sitting in a saucer on his desk. Throwing down the pen, which he had been using, and shoving the teeth into his mouth, he started again. "Is it, Jason?" Mr Jenks asked in a tone which made it clear that he wasn't a happy chap. "It's anything but good. In fact, it's the worst morning of my life so far."

Making my way towards him, I sensed an aura of stress radiating from his huge frame. I paused as he took a slurp from a tea-stained mug before slamming the empty cup down on his desk.

"Anything I can help with?" I asked, hopefully.

"Not unless you can magic up a few thousand pounds by the end of today," he sarcastically snapped. We both looked at each other as an awkward silence hung over us like a storm cloud.

After a few seconds of thinking over what he had said,

the old man shook his head and apologised. "Sorry Jason, I didn't mean to take things out on you. I'm a bit stressed to say the least. To cut a long story short, I need cash and I need it fast. Otherwise today will be the last day I can open the shop."

My heart sank and disappointment filled my body. Apart from school and home, this was the only other place I ever went to, and the thought of it closing sickened me. "There must be something we can do," I desperately pleaded.

Leaning forward, the old man reached out and placed his hand gently on my shoulder. Forcing a smile which allowed his mouth to emerge from his bushy beard, he gave a look which failed to disguise the pain he was feeling inside. Removing his crooked glasses, he wiped his eyes before he pushed them back on and let out a deep sigh. "The best thing you can do to help me is to go and sort through the new stock which I have collected. It's all piled up in the back room. I would appreciate that, so that I can carry on trying to find a way out of this mess."

Nodding, I navigated my way through the cluttered piles which formed a narrow pathway through the shop. Opening the door, I reached round the corner to flick on the light switch and stepped inside the storeroom.

It was at that moment that I spotted it. Initially, it was the colourful stickers on the old, battered, blue suitcase which caught my eye as it sat amid a scene of carnage. Heading straight towards it, I pulled the case free of the surrounding debris and sat myself down on the floor with my back against the wall.

Placing the suitcase on my knee, I tried to pull the lid

open. It was firmly closed and, judging by the catches and keyholes on the front, could have been locked too. Placing my thumbs on the buttons either side of the locks, I slid my thumbs sideways. The locks clicked and the catches flicked open. My heart jumped and my mind raced. This had happened many times when I had been in the same situation and I usually ended up disappointed. Most times I discovered moth-eaten clothes or broken ornaments. But something inside told me this time would be different.

Lifting the lid and allowing it to flop over onto my knees, I looked inside and the sight which met my eyes caused a rush of excitement which surged through my body like a tidal wave. Reaching into the bottom of the case, I picked out a necklace. It was a heavy, gold chain with a silver skull pendant hanging from it. The skull's eyes were filled with what looked like red rubies and the mouth had green jewels which twinkled in the light. I couldn't take my eyes off the skull's wicked grin and it felt as though it was speaking to me. This may sound crazy, but I tell you this with all honesty. The skull was calling out to me and encouraging me to try the necklace on!

Placing the suitcase on the floor, I stood up and slipped the necklace over my head, allowing the skull pendant to sit on my T-shirt. I surveyed the pile of junk and spotted a broken shaving mirror. Picking the mirror up, I inspected my discovery. It was beautiful, but my thoughts switched to its value. This could be the answer to Mr Jenks's financial problems. Judging by the weight of the necklace, it had to be valuable, so I hurriedly pulled the door open to share my find with Mr Jenks.

As I burst from the storeroom, I stopped dead in my tracks. Mr Jenks was no longer sitting at his desk. He had vanished, just like the piles of junk, which had been replaced by a room with long, timber beams along the walls and floor. The front window of the shop had disappeared and the only light entering the room was from three small vents high up in the wall. A door was set in the left hand wall and a heavy wooden table sat in the centre of the room. I couldn't work out what was happening. Where was I?

Heading straight for the door, I pulled at the metal handle, which wouldn't budge an inch. I tried again and still it wouldn't shift. I was locked in!

Moving across the room, I could feel my level of panic rapidly increasing. Half-empty bottles containing a foul-smelling liquid sat on the table, along with a huge map which lay open and took up most of the space. As I scanned the map to try and find a clue as to my whereabouts, I spotted something which struck fear into my heart. In the centre of the map was a dagger which had been stabbed through the map and into the table. Leaning over to inspect the weapon further, I could see dried blood crusted on the blade. Wherever I was, it wasn't somewhere that I should be and I was clearly in extreme danger!

Backing away from the table, I spotted a filthy, green bag on the floor next to the table. Lifting the bag up and holding it above the table, I tipped out the contents. My eyes bulged at the sight of gold coins tumbling like a metallic waterfall onto the map. I looked at the markings as I sifted through the coins, but they looked nothing like the money I was used to seeing. For a start, they were larger and heavier and the Queen's head was nowhere to be seen.

It was at that moment that I heard voices and the sound of a key entering the lock in the door. Shoving a coin into my pocket, I spun around to face the door, just in time to see it swing open and crash against the wall. As I stared in disbelief, I tried to take in what I was seeing. Standing in the doorway, and virtually filling it due to his colossal frame, was a pirate!

"Who be you?" growled the man, in a voice which was filled with threat but also tinged with shock and surprise. "And what be you doing in my cabin?"

The man's eyes flitted around the room before settling on the table behind me. Moving his head to gain a better view, he spotted the sea of coins which I had poured onto the table. "You've been raiding my stash, you thieving dog!"

Moving towards me in a menacing manner, I watched his long, black coat flap open and I spotted he only had one leg as the other, a wooden limb, clonked and clunked on the wooden floor. Before I could move or react, he was face to face with me and grabbed hold of my T-shirt with his shovel-sized hands.

The first thing that hit me was the pungent smell of his breath, which knocked me sick. His eyes were cold and hard and stared at me without ever seeming to blink. The crafted beard only partially hid a road map of scars which travelled the length and breadth of his face. Growling like an angry bear, he watched me intently as I whimpered and quivered as I searched for something to say.

"Nobody steals from Deep Scar Davies!" he growled after what had seemed like an eternal period of silence.

"And most definitely not a scrawny little rat like you!"

Gathering together every ounce of bravery and courage in my traumatised body, I answered him. "I'm Jason. I haven't taken anything from you. I only want to go home."

Lifting me up so that my feet were clear of the floor, he stared at me. "You want to go home do you, little rat?" Swinging me around, he began to make his way back to the door before launching me outside into the blinding sunshine.

It took a few seconds for my eyes to adjust from the gloomy cabin to the brightness, but as they did I hastily scanned my surroundings. Tall masts reached up into the blue sky and huge, black sails billowed out in the wind. Men milled about, some were mopping and sweeping while others carried cargo around. Looking back to the sails, my eye followed the mast to the top where a black and white flag flapped in the wind. It was a skull and crossbones and sent a clear warning to others that this was a ship to be avoided at all costs.

On hearing the disturbance, some of the men had abandoned what they were doing and had begun to move towards me. Deep Scar also moved in my direction and stood over me, glaring down at me as I cowered on the deck.

The men who had gathered, chattered and pointed until Deep Scar raised his hand in the air and they fell silent. "Looks like we have a problem with thieving rats on board," he growled in my direction. "Well boys, we know what we do with rats, don't we?"

The men cheered and punched the air as they began to

chant, "Plank, plank, plank!" It was repeated over and over, gradually getting louder and more spite-filled as the men whipped themselves up into a frenzy.

Reaching down and grabbing the necklace, Deep Scar eyed the skull pendant carefully. "No point throwing this in the sea too," he said as he lifted the necklace over my head before he heaved me up from the deck and dragged me towards the side of the boat.

Spotting a long, thin strip of wood which jutted out from the side of the boat, I realised where things were heading. "Get up there, you filthy rat," barked Deep Scar, as he hoisted me over the side of the boat and dropped me onto the plank of wood. The other pirates excitedly whooped and hollered in the background.

After regaining my feet, I stood on the plank with my arms stretched out like a trapeze artist as the plank wobbled uncontrollably. Behind me Deep Scar stood on the plank and pulled a cutlass from his belt. Jabbing the point into my back, he pushed me along the flexing piece of wood which dipped lower with my every step.

Looking down at the sea below me, I spotted dark silhouettes gliding along beneath the waves. Suddenly, a fin cut the surface of the water. Sharks! The water below was infested and there were more arriving by the second.

Out of the corner of my eye, I saw one of the pirate crew throwing something from a bucket into the water, which seemed to be attracting the beasts. They were feeding the sharks and I knew what the main course was going to be!

"Oh they're hungry today, but I am sure they have plenty of room left for a tasty, little morsel like you!" Deep Scar shouted in a cruel, mocking tone.

By now I had edged my way so far along the plank that the toes of my trainers were hanging off the end. It was taking me all my time to remain upright, and I was running out of plank and ideas. I had to do something quickly, otherwise there would be one of three outcomes. I would either drown, be eaten by the sharks or very possibly both!

Spinning around and swiping my arm at Deep Scar's cutlass, I caught the brute off-guard. The weapon slipped from his grasp and spun up into the air before it dropped down into the clear, blue ocean.

With an expression of hatred and surprise, Deep Scar began to teeter and topple as his feet slipped on the wet plank. He frantically tried to regain his balance, but he was fighting a losing battle. Spotting the necklace still in his hand, I grabbed my opportunity and swiped it from his grasp before slipping it over my head.

Deep Scar continued his out of control pirouettes and twirls on the perilous plank. Suddenly, his feet betrayed him and he fell backwards, striking his head on the plank with a sickening thud before he plunged into the water below.

The circling sharks didn't need a second invitation. The ravenous beasts instantly turned the sea into a frothing feeding frenzy which stained the foaming water into a blood red pool. The pirates booed and jeered from the ship's deck. They waved their fists and drew their weapons as they made their displeasure clear.

All of a sudden, my trainers slipped and I felt myself begin to fall backwards. As I tumbled towards the ocean, I closed my eyes and braced myself for the splashdown which would signal the end.

Fortunately, the end never came. Instead, I opened my eyes to find myself sat in the storeroom once again. The skull pendant was still hanging from my neck, so I removed it and stood up. Holding my breath, I opened the door and looked out.

Mr Jenks sat at his desk. He was still frantically scribbling and scrawling in his search for the answer to his financial problems. The piles of junk were stacked up in every available space, just as they had been when I had first entered the shop.

Walking over to his desk, I put down the skull necklace and waited for a reaction. Mr Jenks picked it up and closely inspected it before placing it back on the desk. "Very pretty indeed," he said, "but I don't think it will be the answer to my problems. It isn't solid gold and the stones are cheap copies. If we get £100 for it we will have done well."

My shoulders must have visibly sagged. I tried to say something which would help, but I found no words to offer any comfort to Mr Jenks. Instead, I trudged towards the door and heard the familiar tinkling bell as I walked out. But before I had let the door shut, I felt something in my pocket which caused me to turn and run back to Mr Jenks.

Placing Deep Scar's gold coin on his desk, I watched as his jaw dropped and his eyes alternated between me and the coin. His face lit up in a way which I had never seen and tears of joy meandered their way down his chubby cheeks. He hugged me tightly and we danced a jig of joy amid the junk and trash.

As for the coin, it was bought by a rich collector from

America and is apparently the only genuine pirate coin in the whole world. More importantly, the money it made proved more than enough to save Mr Jenks's shop. He is still running it to this day and recently even treated himself to a new sign.

As for me, I now have an endless supply of friends after our story featured in the local and national papers. My friends never seem to tire of my story about Deep Scar Davies and the pirate pendant.

BOOTED OUT

Rain drizzled from the slate grey sky as Mr Watts, our football coach, stood in front of us with his arms folded and a blank expression on his face. He scanned the line of saturated, yet hopeful, individuals standing before him in the middle of the flooded fields of St Martin's School.

Nervous glances were exchanged as each boy waited to discover if their dream of playing for the school team would remain alive, or alternatively, be squashed for another year.

Plodding through the ankle-deep mud, Mr Watts moved toward the expectant line. Each boy nervously squelched and shuffled in the mud bath of a field as the teacher simply smiled and nodded or shook his head. Broad smiles and fist pumps broke out from some, frowns and drooped shoulders from others.

The decider of fate had now reached me, and in my heart I knew what the outcome would be. It would undoubtedly be the same conclusion which had been reached every other year I had tried out for the team. Looking me square in the eye, Mr Watts reached out with his hand and touched my shoulder. "Not this year, Pete," Mr Watts explained with as much sympathy as he could create in his voice. "Well done for turning up and giving it your best shot, but I honestly don't think you are ready for the team yet."

Forcing a smile and nodding my head in faked agreement, I replied, "No worries, Sir." On the outside I seemed to take the rejection really well, but on the inside, I was devastated. My dreams were in tatters yet again. To be honest, after all these years of knock-backs, maybe I had to admit that my chances of making the team were slim to non-existent!

As I trudged back to the changing rooms, the torrential rain still poured from the heavy sky. The raindrops mixed with my salty tears to create a cascading river which flowed down my flushed, red cheeks. Ahead of me, I could hear the excited chatter emerging from the changing room, which just worsened the feeling of frustration that burned inside me. I desperately wanted to be part of the football team, but fate did not seem to be on my side and the dream was fading so fast, it was barely still visible.

"Hey Pete, sorry you didn't make the team again," Brad said sympathetically, putting his arm around my shoulder. "Fancy a milkshake on the way home? My shout?"

Brad was one of the nicest kids in my class and had been my best mate since we started school together years ago. We were like brothers in so many ways, or at least until it came to football. He was an absolute soccer superstar and the team captain, whereas I was the annual team reject and next door to useless.

"Not tonight, but thanks though," I replied. "I have to visit Grandad on the way home."

After showering and changing, I rammed my filthy kit into my bag and was heading out of the now-deserted changing rooms when I spotted Mr Watts. He was removing some tatty pieces of paper from the notice board, but stopped when he saw me.

"Hello Pete. Well done again for trying out for the team,

maybe football just isn't your thing. I'm starting a table tennis club soon, take a flyer and see what you think," he said, as he pushed a piece of paper into my hand.

My heart sank even further, if that was physically possible. Scrunching up the paper and pushing it into my pocket, I nodded to Mr Watts and walked out onto the yard. After checking that he was out of sight, I tossed the flyer into the bin. Maybe I had to listen to the advice and accept what he was saying; I just wasn't cut out for football.

Making my way down the high street, with the rain now turning to drizzle, I spotted the blue and white sign which marked Grandad's nursing home. He had been ill for a while now. Mum had tried her best to look after him, but she couldn't manage so she'd decided that he would receive the best care in a nursing home. It wasn't a bad sort of place and the nurses were all lovely and caring, but I had noticed that Grandad had lost his old sparkle since he had moved in. The staff undoubtedly did a great job, but that shine in his eyes had faded badly in the last few months and I didn't like seeing it happen one bit.

"Hey Grandad," I said as I tapped on the door of his room, before wandering in and sitting down on the chair next to him. The old man slowly turned his head and a gentle smile crept across his face. He raised his hand and took mine, his dull eyes becoming teary. I spent the next few minutes telling him about the events of the afternoon and reliving the painful rejection yet again. Grandad watched and listened, not uttering a word.

Grandad's memory was getting tired, or that was at least how Mum had explained it to me. She had used a really long, complicated word which I had never heard of, so I preferred to think of it as him getting forgetful. He tended to ask the same questions over and over, needed lots of reminders about the simplest things and often took a long time to remember what he wanted to say.

"I wasn't much good at football when I was at school either," Grandad unexpectedly remarked. "I got turned down for the team every year." I listened intently, not wanting to break his thought process while he was on a roll and making sense. "Eventually though, I made it," he explained. He slowly turned his head, so that his eyes were dead in line with my own. "I put it all down to a special present," he secretively whispered.

Without warning, he rose to his feet and shuffled across the room, his slippers sliding across the polished, tiled floor. Opening the wardrobe doors, he bent forward and removed a package, before returning to his original seated position.

On his knee sat an old, battered cardboard box coated in layers of dust. Brushing at the dust with one hand, he began to open the box with the other. I leaned forward in my seat, intrigued to know what was about to be revealed.

"What have you got there?" I asked him inquisitively.

"Go and shut the door and I'll tell you," he instructed in a firm voice. "What I am about to tell you must never be repeated to another soul. Do you understand?"

After pushing the door shut, I nodded in reply and

darted back to my seat as I hung on the old man's every word.

Grandad gently slid the lid completely off the box to reveal a pair of football boots. They were like nothing I had ever seen. The boots were made from faded, brown leather with long, rusty, metal studs, some of which were missing. The laces were black and fraying and looked like they had seen better days and would snap if someone tried to tie them. These boots were ancient!

"They were given to me by my Mum when I was about your age," he whispered. "They must be nearly 90 years old. She bought them for me from an old second hand shop in town. I wore them every time I played, but I think my playing days are long gone now. I want you to have them. They might bring you a bit of luck."

"Wow, thanks," I replied taking the box from Grandad and further inspecting the ancient boots. "I promise I will look after them and they will always remind me of you."

A lonely tear trickled its way down the old man's cheek and disappeared into his thick beard. He lifted his hand and affectionately ruffled my hair. "Just remember though, they are special boots, so look after them well," he advised before returning his gaze to the sky and clouds through the window.

Pushing the box into my kitbag, I wrapped my arms around Grandad and placed a tender kiss on his wrinkled forehead. His vacant eyes continued to stare out of the window, so I quietly left him in peace and crept out of the door.

That evening, I lay on my bed with Grandad's boots next to me. I carefully inspected them, running my fingers across the stitches, feeling the leather and the jagged edges of the worn studs. I thought about Grandad and all the goals he would have scored when he was a boy. How I wished that I could do the same! Before turning in for the night, I carefully placed the boots into the box and pushed them into my kitbag. I was desperate to show Brad, although part of me wanted to respect Grandad's wish for secrecy.

My sleep that night was different to most. I had dreams filled with football, with me scoring goals and dancing joyfully on the pitch. It was amazing!

At least it was until I was jolted awake in the middle of the night by the phone noisily ringing. I sat up in the darkness and listened as Mum's voice became more and more distressed. As soon as the call had ended, footsteps bounded up the stairs and my bedroom door flew open, the landing light chasing away the darkness.

"Pete, Pete," Mum hissed in a voice which bordered on frantic. "Grandad has been rushed into hospital. I need to go straight away. He's struggling to breathe, according to the nurse."

My mind began to race and I choked back tears. "Is he going to…?" I asked, not having the heart to finish the sentence.

Mum knew what I was asking and didn't answer the question. "You help me by sorting yourself out," she instructed. "Love you." She switched off the light and closed the door.

Before I had chance to reply, Mum had gone and her footsteps disappeared off across the landing. Within minutes the car fired up and I was alone. I lay silently in bed, knowing that sleep wouldn't come easily. All I could think of were the beautiful moments I had shared with Grandad earlier. Would they ever be repeated? Tears flowed down my face as the negative thoughts flooded my head like an emotional dam had burst.

Eventually, morning came and I wearily hauled myself out of bed. The first thing which struck me was just how eerily silent the house was. Never had I felt so alone and never had I been so glad to get to school to have some familiar faces and voices around me. That day was never-ending, and with all that had happened I had totally forgotten about the football match until Brad reminded me.

"Coming to watch the match tonight?" he asked. "It might take your mind off other things."

"I suppose you're right," I reluctantly replied. "I'll be there."

The rest of the day dragged terribly. Teachers talked, but nothing entered my head as it was so full of concerns and worries and there was no room for anything else. The end of school bell brought me crashing back to the land of the living as I trudged across the yard and flopped down on the concrete bench next to the pitch.

Brad was the first player to appear from the changing

rooms, followed by Smudger Sutton, Alfie Parkes and last of all Tom and Andy Gritt. The team chatted excitedly as I sat alone, in my own distant world.

A voice suddenly thundered out of nowhere, "Pete! Pete!" Tuning my mind back into the real world, I spotted Mr Watts frantically dashing across the yard, clutching his clipboard and wearing a concerned expression on his face. "I realise this is a long shot," he said trying to gather his breath, "but have you got your boots?"

Shooting a puzzled expression back at Mr Watts, I replied, "My boots? Why would I need my boots? I'm here to watch, not to play. Does someone need to borrow them?"

"Not really," he replied. "I need them on your feet and I need you on that pitch. Asa Edwards has gone home sick and we're a player short. The game can't go ahead as things stand." Mr Watts looked at me with the look of a desperate man who had no other options. I was clearly his final call.

I took a minute to process what was happening and then groaned out loud. My boots were at home as I had left them with my dirty kit in the kitchen. Heartbreak! Unbelievable! Then an idea entered my head. "Give me two minutes and I'll be ready," I said, grabbing my bag and pelting across the yard to the changing rooms.

Well I can't explain how incredible it felt to pull on the orange and white top, white shorts and black socks. My head spun with excitement, and the sadness of what had happened last night eased a little.

"Are you ready yet, Pete?" Mr Watts anxiously asked as he popped his head into the changing room.

"Nearly," I replied, "I just need to put my boots on." Reaching into my bag, I pulled out Grandad's boots and pushed my feet into them. A perfect fit! Amazing! As I began to lace them up, a warm sensation began to travel up my legs and the hairs stood on end. At first, I put it down to the excitement of everything that was going on, but as it gradually swept over my body, I accepted there was more to it. It was a feeling I had never experienced before. I shoved my shin pads down my socks and confidently strode onto the pitch.

It was at this point that everyone else saw me and my boots and I was met with a chorus of laughter, especially from the opposition. "Look at his boots," mocked a tall boy with long hair. "Have you been to a charity shop for those?"

"Mummy not able to afford any decent boots?" mocked another short, stocky boy. The pack of boys cackled like hysterical hyenas.

"Ignore them, Pete," encouraged Brad, patting me on the back. "Just stay near the goal and if the ball comes to you, try and score." I simply nodded at Brad. My whole body was now tingling and buzzing uncontrollably. I felt super-fast and super-confident.

The match kicked off and I charged down the pitch. Usually I plodded along, at best, but today I scooted over the grass and my feet barely seemed to touch the floor.

Suddenly the ball zipped past me and I chased it down, moving like a bullet fired from a gun. The goalkeeper stood his ground, towering like a skyscraper and seeming to fill the goal with his body. With supreme confidence, I pulled back my boot and flicked the ball up over his head, leaving him grasping at thin air and the ball trickling into the empty net. The celebrations were epic and I was mobbed by my team-mates, who danced and cheered. This was the stuff of dreams and I was feeling immense!

Minutes later, I picked up the ball on the halfway line and kicked it with every ounce of power my foot could muster. The ball swerved and curled in the air before it arrowed into the top corner of the net, leaving the keeper sprawled out on the muddy field. Brad grabbed me and we danced a jig of ultimate joy and delight. As I looked across the pitch, I could see Mr Watts on the sideline shaking his head, a totally baffled expression on his face. He had never seen anything like this!

Well the rest, as they say, is history, and although I didn't score any more goals, we went on to win the game with ease. The final whistle was greeted with uncontrollable delight and wild celebrations, which left the boys who had previously mocked me, walking off the pitch scratching their heads as they tried to work out what had gone on.

"Amazing performance today," exclaimed Mr Watts as he patted me on the back. "Must have been your lucky boots I guess," he added. "Plus, I think it is lovely that you had someone special watching your incredible performance."

As I slowly turned around, my eyes fell upon an amazing sight. Sitting on the bench by the side of the pitch was Mum, and by her side, wearing a smile of total pride, was Grandad. I sprinted over and threw my arms around them both. "How are you feeling, Grandad?" I asked.

"Much better now that I have seen my old boots haven't lost their magic touch," he said, with a cheeky smile and a knowing wink.

DON'T BELIEVE YOUR EYES

Mum and Dad sat in complete silence, staring angrily at each other with looks which said more than words ever could. Things hadn't been going well for a while, but this stand-off had taken things to a new level and had created a horrible atmosphere which I didn't like one bit. Dad began to clear his throat and tried to break the silence, but nothing came out.

Mum huffed loudly and rose to her feet from the battered armchair where she had been defiantly perched. Trudging through to the kitchen, slippers sliding across the threadbare lounge carpet, she flicked the kettle on before letting loose another frustrated sigh.

Without alerting either of them to the fact that I had been spying on them, I rose from my seated position on the stairs and tiptoed down the remaining steps, before I waltzed into the lounge pretending that I had seen nothing.

Dad sat in his chair, staring blankly out of the window with his glasses perched on the end of his nose. As he spotted me, he quickly wiped his eyes and pushed the glasses back up his nose. He was clearly upset, but Dad was not a man who showed his emotions, especially in front of his daughter. Rising from his chair, he held out his arms before wrapping them around me and tenderly kissing my head.

"You're upset, Dad," I pointed out in a concerned voice. Sighing deeply, he pulled back and looked me in the eye. Large teardrops filled the corners of his eyes.

"You shouldn't have to see this, Felicity," he apologised weakly. "This isn't your problem." One of the teardrops trickled down his right cheek, causing him to wipe it away before it had made much progress and, more importantly, been spotted by me.

"If I can help in any way, you know I will," I urged, secretly hoping for a simple solution, which in my heart I knew wouldn't come.

"Well unless you have £1,000 in your piggy bank, I don't think you can do much, unfortunately. We have real money problems and we're struggling to make the repayments on the house this month. Things don't look good," he explained in a voice which was filled with sadness.

Taking a couple of steps back, I looked at him with a confused expression. "Are we going to have to move again? I can't leave my friends. This can't keep happening!" Dad broke eye contact with me and his head sank lower before he turned his face away.

I ran up the stairs two at a time, bursting through my bedroom door and slumping onto my bed. I angrily wiped away tears and fiercely cursed the whole situation. This couldn't be happening all over again. It was like a recurring nightmare which we just kept living through. Why do other people have money and nice things, while we struggle from day to day to make ends meet? Rolling over, I looked across at my bedside clock and realised that it was twenty minutes until school start time.

I wiped at my eyes before I reached over to grab my can

of hairspray. If I was going to be late, at least I could look presentable, and my wild mane needed taming before I went out in public!

Walking over to the mirror, I began to empty the contents of the aerosol can on my hair when I was met with the dreaded hissing noise which signalled the can was empty. I furiously launched the can across the room and began to pull open one drawer after another in search of a new can. After raiding every drawer, I accepted temporary defeat.

Heading across the landing, I thundered into my parents' room and began to rummage through Mum's cupboard. Nothing of use at all! Could this morning get any worse? Just as I was about to push the cupboard doors shut, I spotted a rusted canister with faded writing, at the back of the cupboard. Taking it out, I inspected it carefully. The writing was barely legible and after numerous attempts, I gave up.

Time was running out, so I raced back across the landing to my bedroom and decided the can I had found was worth a try. Bending my head forward and allowing my hair to hang down, I began to spray. The contents of the can didn't smell any different to the usual hairspray I used, but what happened next was anything but normal.

Raising my head, I flicked my long hair back and looked in the mirror. What I saw horrified me! It chilled me to the bone! Staring back at me from the mirror was a headless body! My mind swirled and my thoughts raced. Raising my empty hand, I went to touch my head and I could most definitely feel the outline, but it felt as if I was touching someone else's head.

Flopping back onto my bed before my legs gave way, I sat on the edge and gathered my thoughts. My mind searched for an answer to the bizarre situation I found myself in. As I looked in the mirror, to my utter disbelief, my head was beginning to reappear before my eyes. It was like watching an artist complete a portrait from the neck up.

Within a couple of minutes, my head was fully restored to the state it had been before I used the mystery spray. I looked from the mirror to the can of spray in my hand. I had stumbled on something which was incredibly powerful, but I knew that Mum and Dad would confiscate it if they found out what it could do. Tossing the spray into my school bag, I rearranged my newly appeared hair and headed to school.

After the mind-boggling craziness of the morning, the day passed without event and before long I was heading home. Strolling along in the blazing sunshine, I turned to my best friend, Simone. The hairspray story had been hard to keep to myself all day and I was desperate to share it, even if I was still struggling to believe it myself.

Simone and I had been friends since I started at Millington School a few months earlier. We had hit it off instantly and we knew each other inside out, becoming firm friends. During our friendship we had shared a lot, including my family's money worries, which had made us stronger. I couldn't bear to think about my family being forced to move on again and dreaded the prospect of leaving Simone and my other friends behind. What I was about to tell Simone would eclipse anything that we had shared before. I knew it would blow her mind, but I had to share my story.

As we entered the park, we threw ourselves down onto the freshly cut grass and dropped our bags. Turning to Simone, I unleashed the secret of a lifetime. "If I show you something that is beyond belief, would you promise to keep it a secret?" I asked pushing my hand into my school bag.

"Yeah, definitely," she replied, looking curious about what I was about to reveal.

Before I pulled the canister out of my school bag, I scanned the park to make sure nobody else was around. Seeing the coast was clear, I placed it on the grass and looked at the baffled expression on Simone's face.

"I know this looks like a normal can," I excitedly explained, "but it is so much more."

With a perplexed expression, Simone looked from the can to me and back to the can, trying to work out what was going on. "Okay, do you want to explain things a little more?" she slowly said.

Without speaking, I flicked the green plastic lid off the can and sprayed a small amount on my hand. Before our eyes, the fingers on my hand began to fade from sight and within seconds, my hand had completely disappeared up to the wrist.

Simone's eyes flitted from the handless limb to the can of spray. Her mouth gaped as she frantically looked around for the mysterious missing hand. "Crikey!" she gasped. "Where's your hand gone? How did you do that? What has just happened? Come on, explain how you did that," she desperately pleaded.

"Give it a few minutes," I replied. "Just keep watching." Simone's eyes were fixed on the end of my arm as we patiently waited. Very slowly, the flesh on the back of my hand began to reappear, followed by my fingers, until the hand had completely returned and was fully restored.

Simone stood up and began to gently shake her head in disbelief while reaching out to feel my hand. I went on to explain the whole episode from this morning to Simone which did nothing apart from further baffle the poor girl. Just as I had finished my explanation, I sensed someone behind us. Turning around, I was faced with a sight which struck fear into me and made me hide the spray can behind my back.

"Well, look who we have here. It's the two girly freaks of Millington School," growled our uninvited guest. It was Todd Wicks, the most cruel child in our school, who was widely recognised as the official school bully. "I am fed up with telling you two little wimps that this is my park and I don't want you here," he hissed, clenching his fists and screwing up his face so that his eyes were narrowed and threatening.

I surreptitiously pushed the spray can into my bag as we

gathered our belongings together and scurried away. Fortunately Todd Wicks didn't follow us and his cruel cackling faded into the distance behind us.

Splitting up at the park gates, we headed our separate ways and I made my way home, hoping the grim atmosphere of the morning would have lifted and some solutions to our money problems may have been discovered.

As it happened, the atmosphere at home was still icy cold and after dinner, which was eaten in virtual silence, I sought sanctuary in my room. Pondering the possible outcomes of our rocky financial situation, I drifted off to sleep, hoping the next day would bring some positives.

The next morning, Simone met me on my way to school. "Are you ready for the science test this afternoon?" she asked. "There's so much to remember that it feels like my brain is going to explode with information overload!"

A combination of stress at home and the excitement of the newly-discovered spray can meant I had totally forgotten about the test. With my grades drastically plummeting lately, I was under lots of pressure to pass this test, or else I would be in serious trouble. "Oh no," I replied.

Suddenly an idea popped into my head and I grabbed Simone's shoulder, which halted her in her tracks. "If you're willing to help me at break, I think I have a way of getting us a little bit of help with this test," I explained.

When morning break arrived, Simone and I made our

way to the science block and headed into the nearby toilets. We both squeezed into a single cubicle and I removed the spray can from my bag and immediately got to work.

A couple of minutes later, the toilet door opened and Simone left, carrying both her bag and mine. I can't explain how it felt to be completely invisible. It was probably best described as a mixture of fear and thrilled excitement. I was buzzing at the prospect of what I could get away with while nobody could see me, but also worried that the effects may not reverse this time and I could be left like this forever!

Sliding through the open classroom door like a ghost, I scanned the room to see Mr Murray, our teacher, sitting at his desk reading his newspaper. The room was otherwise deserted. Lying at the back of the class were the separate pages of the test paper. Like a thief in the night, I made my way over and looked at each page in turn, making a note in my head of the topics which were covered. Mr Murray continued to read his paper, totally oblivious to the presence of the invisible invader who was only feet from him.

As I looked at the final sheet, I noticed something which sent a jolt of fear through my body. The thumb on my right hand was clearly visible and I realised the spray's effects were wearing off. As I turned around to make my escape, Miss Smith appeared in the doorway, blocking my route to safety. To my horror, she began a conversation with Mr Murray. My fingers and thumb had now reappeared and were quickly being followed by the back of my hand.

There was nothing left but to hide until the coast was clear. Spotting the stockroom door propped open, I headed over, just as the back of my hand and lower arm made an appearance. Taking cover in the darkness of the stockroom, I was just in time as my arms and chest were now clearly visible. As I inspected the rest of my body, I noticed a large section of my stomach had reappeared and it dawned on me that the parts of the body which I sprayed first were also the first to return. Seeing that the teachers were still chatting, I realised it was now a matter of staying put and hoping that they didn't come and discover my hiding place.

Fortunately both teachers left after a couple of minutes, which cleared my escape route. Leaving the room, I saw Simone stood anxiously waiting and I gave her a thumbs up to signal my success. We headed out onto the yard, where I explained everything I had seen during my secret mission.

Well, needless to say, we both passed the test with flying colours and Mr Murray was none the wiser to our outrageous plan. As we happily strolled out of the school gates, we noticed a large group of children gathered around in an excited huddle. Making our way over, I spotted something pinned on the school notice board. I jostled with the crowd to get a spot where I could see what the fuss was all about. Eventually, I saw the bold print at the top of a white sheet of paper, which read, 'Hide and Seek National Championship'.

The rest of the sheet explained where the event was to be held, the rules and most importantly the prize, which was

£1,000 in cash. I realised this could be the answer to all of our problems and knew straight away I had to enter and win. I also knew a way that I could get a real advantage on the other competitors.

That night, I found the application form on the website and entered my details. Extra information on the website explained how entries would be picked at random and not all of the children would be successful, as numbers were limited. Clicking the 'Enter' button, I crossed my fingers and hoped for the best.

For the next few days, time seemed to go backwards and every morning and evening I would check my inbox, but it remained empty apart from the odd junk message which I frustratedly trashed.

On Thursday evening I logged in to find a message which read, 'Congratulations! Are you ready to hide and seek?' My heart skipped a beat as I clicked it open. I couldn't read fast enough, but straight away understood I had been one of the fortunate ones to be selected! At last I had received a lucky break. Little did I realise that my joy would be short-lived.

As I was heading across the yard the next morning, I noticed a crowd gathered again around the poster. This time there was no excited chatter as the children stood in silence as Todd Wicks spoke to his assembled audience. "So it looks like I have this competition in the bag," he explained, pointing to the poster. "I have been given one of the places and my Dad has agreed to pay a soldier from the army to train me up in camouflage skills. I will be unbeatable!" My hopes plummeted and my heart sank. The last person I wanted to face was Todd, especially with supposed experts training him up. It would be impossible to find him.

Settling myself on a bench to catch some early morning sun, I placed my bag by my side and waited for Simone. Unfortunately my peaceful moment was short-lived as my bag rocketed up in the air and landed on the yard. The contents scattered everywhere and I sprang to my feet to gather them together and see who was responsible.

"What have we got here?" growled a familiar voice. "Think I'll keep this, it looks interesting," snarled Todd Wicks, holding the can of hairspray in the air.

"Give that back," I said, snatching at the out of reach can. I watched helplessly as he dropped the can into his bag and headed off across the yard. Unsurprisingly, my desperate pleas were met with mocking laughter and the realisation that my secret weapon was gone.

Gathering the remaining contents of my bag together, I followed Todd to the PE changing rooms and waited around the corner for the boys to change and head out onto the field. Once they had gone, I slipped into the changing room and began to search for Todd's bag. Just as I found it, I heard voices getting closer. The boys were back early!

Without thinking it through, I uncapped the can and began to cover myself from head to toe. I instantly began to disappear. My left foot completed the disappearing act just as the door swung open and a pack of muddy and wet boys burst in. What happened next left me in shock! The boys began to strip off their muddy kit and before long I stood in the middle of a room full of muddy, sweaty boys, and worst of all they were all naked! Trying to avert my gaze away from you know where, I hurried out through the open door and away. That was a close call, but at least I had my secret weapon back and I had time to prepare for the big day next weekend.

When the day finally arrived, I nervously made my way onto our school fields which would be the venue for the event. Children milled around and I spotted Todd Wicks strutting confidently around as if he thought he had it nailed. The rules were explained by a man with a loud hailer and we were told that we had to stay out of sight from a team of older children for as long as possible, the last one remaining undiscovered would be the winner.

A loud hooter sounded, and we headed off into the woods to search for a hiding place. Several minutes later it sounded again, to signal the release of the 'seekers'.

Splitting from the rest of the pack, I found a small clearing and took out the spray before covering myself from head to toe. Seconds after I had finished, the seekers raced past me as if I were not there. Perfect! My plan was up and running and working like a treat.

Whistles sounded around the woods, signalling the capture of competitors. I counted the whistles and when I had heard eight, I knew that there was only one more competitor remaining besides myself. I also had a feeling I knew who that would be.

Looking down at my feet, I realised the effects of the spray were wearing off. As the glorious sunshine streamed down I applied a fresh coat of spray. I looked through the bushes just in time to see the pack of seekers heading towards me. Freezing like a statue, I watched them as they passed by without any of them detecting my presence. I felt so confident that I even stuck my tongue out at them! Without warning, they began to shout and whoop and changed direction. Something had caught their attention.

Observing through the bushes, I watched the seekers head off with the scent of a capture in their nostrils. A short while later, a chorus of whistles sounded as they led Todd Wicks out of the woodland arena. I had remained hidden and the victory was mine! Allowing my body time to reappear, I emerged from my hiding place and was greeted by a cheering crowd which surged forward to congratulate me.

There was one person who of course didn't want to celebrate my success and that was Todd Wicks. He stormed over and pushed children aside as his raging temper took control of his actions.

Before I could react, his hand slipped inside my coat pocket and pulled out the spray can. The crowd watched and awaited the outcome of the confrontation. Holding up the spray can for the crowd to see, he began to rant, "Freaky Felicity has used this to cheat her way to the win. I think I know how, and I am going to prove it."

As rain began to drizzle down, Todd pulled the lid off the can and began to spray the contents over himself. I tried to stop him, I honestly did. "Stop! You can't mix that stuff with ..." I never finished the sentence, because Todd had already covered himself with the spray. Unfortunately I didn't get to mention the word 'water'. You see, the only part of the writing I could make out on the can gave a strict warning in bold text that the spray must not be used in wet conditions. By now, rain was tipping down.

What happened next will stick in my mind for eternity. Rather than disappear, Todd's long, greasy hair began to fall out in clumps, followed by his eyebrows which fluttered onto the muddy grass. He screamed in horror and threw the can to the floor as the rain turned even heavier. The crowd stepped back, just in time to see his clothes begin to disintegrate and drop to the ground which left him totally naked and frantically trying to cover up his modesty! The crowd erupted into fits of laughter. Desperate to escape, he turned and made a run for it, his bare bottom bouncing up and down as he fled.

Although I did feel a little guilty for cheating, I knew that I did it for the right reasons. The prize money paid off our debts, which meant we no longer had to worry about losing the house and being forced to move on. As for Todd Wicks, he didn't trouble anyone ever again!

DO AS THEY DO

The waves gently lapped onto the golden sand and made their way up the beach a little way, before gently dropping back to where their journey had begun. Gulls screamed and screeched their noisy conversations while hovering on the breeze which gently pushed along the cotton wool clouds in the endless, blue sky.

Down below, a lone figure slowly moved across the golden sand. Head down and listening intently through a pair of headphones while moving a metal rod across the sand, Sam searched. She had performed this routine each day of every school holiday, for as long as she could recall during her stays with Uncle Rod. Sam's metal detector was her most prized possession, and searching endlessly on the beach was her only escape from the chaos that was Uncle Rod's life. It gave her a few hours of peace and calm, and allowed her time to recharge before she faced the challenges which staying with him delivered.

Sam listened intently and waited for the slightest bleep which would signal a discovery. Stepping over assorted debris and junk which had been delivered by the sea, she worked her way up the beach. Moving the metal detector one way, then the other, she allowed it to gently pass over the surface of the sand.

Without warning, the needle on the detector's dial began to excitedly swing back and forth. A high-pitched squeal in her earphones made her jump with a combination of shock and excitement. Placing the metal detector on the warm sand, Sam took the rucksack from her back and removed a small shovel. She started to dig in the area where the signal had come from.

As Sam cut through the soft sand and piled it next to the hole she was creating, she recalled past 'treasures' she had discovered, which included rusted drink cans and twisted fishing hooks. It was due to these wasted outings that Sam didn't hold much hope this time. Breaking off for a breather, Sam scraped back her long, blonde hair and placed a cap from her bag onto her head to give some protection from the unforgiving sun which was beating down.

After another stint of digging, she suddenly stopped as her shovel hit something hard. Sam leaned into the hole and began to scrape the sand away with her hands to reveal a wooden object. Pulling the find from its resting place, Sam lifted it out of the hole and placed it on the beach where she dusted it down to reveal a wooden box.

The box was heavy and covered in a strange carved pattern which she inspected carefully. There was a metal clasp on the front of the box which was keeping it securely shut. Using all her force, Sam tried in vain to open it, but the lid would not budge. Holding the box in the air and placing her left ear close to it, she moved it gently from side to side.

Sam could hear something rattling inside the box. Her expectation levels went through the roof and she knew she had to discover what the box contained. Stuffing the sandy object into her rucksack, she excitedly headed back to Uncle

Rod's beach house.

Pushing the door open, she prepared herself for the chaotic scene which would greet her. As she walked in, she used her foot to push aside the pile of mail which had built up and was now scattered all over the floor. The table next to the window in the lounge was stacked high with junk, some of which had toppled and cascaded onto the filthy sofa. Empty bottles, cans and plates were scattered across the floor, creating a minefield of garbage. The place was an absolute bomb site! As Sam stepped forward, her foot caught a bottle which sent it crashing noisily onto a food-encrusted plate.

From a battered, old chair in the corner of the room, Uncle Rod stirred. Leaning forward with his eyes wide open and arms outstretched, the old man took a few seconds to come to terms with his sudden awakening. Trying to work out what was happening and where he was, he mumbled and groaned as he sat up, rubbing his eyes. He scratched at his thinning, grey hair before raking through his beard with his cigarette-stained fingers. Smiling at Sam, he revealed a single gravestone tooth at the front of his gummy mouth. Rod leaned forward and reached out for a crutch which was propped against the wall, but it was just out of his reach. Letting out an agonising groan, he slumped back in the chair.

Lifting the rucksack from her back and placing it on the litter-strewn sofa, Sam perched on the arm of the sofa and took the old man's bony hand. "You can't keep going on like this, Uncle Rod," Sam urged as the old man winced at the pain which was coursing through his deteriorating body.

Screwing his face up as he tried in vain to deal with the agony, Rod repositioned himself in the chair and let out a sigh. "I'm struggling this morning, Sam. My back and legs are killing me. It's taken me ages to get going. I'm just glad you were here to help me out of bed and into my chair before you went off," he groaned. Sam gripped the old man's hand even more tightly and forced a smile.

"There must be something someone can do to help," said Sam.

"The doctors reckon there is nothing more they can do for me. They've tried everything they know. I just have to deal with the pain and not being able to move very well. They want me to give up my beach house and move into a nursing home," he said sadly, turning his face away from Sam. "It looks like I'll go into the Tall Trees Nursing Home tomorrow," he added as tears began to flow down his whiskery cheeks before disappearing into his thick, tangled beard. "I didn't want to upset you by telling you."

"No! I won't let that happen," protested Sam. "I'll stay and look after you, or you can come and stay with me and Mum."

Turning back to face Sam, Rod clutched the girl's hand and looked her in the eyes. The old man's spirit was broken and he was clearly defeated and had accepted his fate.

"Well if you won't fight, I will," said Sam angrily. "I'll think of something." Grabbing her rucksack before heading out into the back garden, Sam made her way to the shed and slid the door open before sitting herself down amid the tools and broken machinery which took up most of the space.

Lifting the wooden box she had found on the beach onto her knee, Sam grabbed a screwdriver and jammed it into the lock. She took all of her frustrations out on the box until she heard a splintering noise as the lock clunked and the surrounding wood gave way, which allowed the lid to pop open. Placing the screwdriver on the floor, Sam lifted the lid of the box and looked in.

The inside of the box had a thick layer of red velvet which cushioned and protected the object which lay within. Sam's eyes grew wide and her mouth gaped as she reached into the box and pulled out a beautiful, golden bangle. Holding it in the light which streamed in through the shed window, she looked carefully at the intricate designs which were cut into the object. There was writing on the inside of the bangle, but it looked like nothing she had ever seen and she couldn't understand a word of it. Polishing the bangle on her T-shirt, she scrunched the fingers on her left hand together and slid the bangle on. It dangled from her wrist and Sam again held it up to the light as she further admired and inspected it. Her mind raced as she thought how much the golden bangle could be worth. It could make her a millionaire!

Placing the broken box on the floor, she locked up the shed and headed across the garden. Opening the back door, she shouted to Rod, "Just going back to the beach, but I won't be long."

"No worries," replied Uncle Rod as Sam pulled the battered door shut and made her way along the cliff top path which led down to the beach.

As she made her way across the golden sand, she heard the buzz of a boat engine and looked out to sea, where she spotted a speedboat zipping along at high speed. Behind the boat was a water-skier, who skipped across the waves before majestically spinning and twirling. Sam's eyes were fixed on the water-skier and it amazed her how effortless it all seemed. As the boat turned to head in the opposite direction, the water-skier stood on one ski and held the towing handle with a single hand. It was amazing, and Sam watched in awe and wonder.

Before long, the boat turned once more and began to head to shore. Sam felt the bite of disappointment as she realised the show was over. Her focus was suddenly diverted though, as she felt a searing, burning pain on the skin where she had the bangle. Shaking her wrist vigorously, she looked at the bangle and for a split-second it appeared to glow before the pain in her wrist eased.

Spotting Sam slumped on the sand, the skier made her way over. "Hey Sam, I saw you watching me. Did you enjoy that? Fancy a go?" Sam recognised the water-skier as Mrs Adams from the nearby village.

Reaching up, Sam took Mrs Adams's hand and shook it firmly. At that moment, a crackle of what seemed like static electricity buzzed between them, making Mrs Adams leap backwards and Sam vigorously shake her hand to gain some relief. "Looks like we're both carrying a bit of a charge," Mrs Adams said, with a smile.

Standing up, Sam looked at the boat. "I've never done this before. I think I might end up drowning," replied Sam.

"Not with one of these," said Mrs Adams, as she handed Sam a life jacket. "You'll love it! Come on, let's get you kitted out."

Sam pulled on a tight-fitting wetsuit, fastened up the life jacket and attached the skis before wading into the water. Floating and bobbing on the gentle waves, as Mrs Adams explained the instructions, Sam watched as she clambered onto the boat to join the driver.

"Straighten your arms," yelled Mrs Adams, fighting against the roar of the boat engine as it revved up and pulled away.

Before Sam knew it, she was upright and scooting across the waves. Mrs Adams gave an enthusiastic thumbs up from the back of the boat, which filled Sam with confidence.

As the boat turned, Sam felt her newly-found confidence surge throughout her body. Lifting one ski clear of the water, she balanced like a ballerina. Mrs Adams pumped her fists in the air and screamed with surprised delight. Growing even more confident, Sam took one hand from the towing handle and waved to a group of people on the beach who squealed with delight and waved back. Sam felt amazing! Having never skied before, she was performing like a professional. Mrs Adams danced around on the boat, hopping from foot to foot.

The boat gradually turned to shore and Sam released the handle before gracefully gliding to land, followed by Mrs Adams who splashed through the water. "Wow, Sam! You were incredible! It has taken me years of practice to be able to ski like that and you did it on your first attempt. How did you pull it off?" Looking at the golden bangle which sat on her wrist, a crazy idea popped into Sam's head which may have answered Mrs Adams's question.

Stripping the ski gear off and putting her clothes back on, Sam thanked Mrs Adams, but knew she needed to check on Uncle Rod as she had been away for a good chunk of the day. Beaming with pride, Sam headed back up to the beach house to find Rod still slumped in his chair. After heating up the contents of a can of soup and toasting some stale bread, Sam helped him with his dinner before supporting him as they slowly made their way through the chaos of the hut to the bedroom. She lay Rod down on his stained duvet and lifted the old man's thin legs up onto the bed.

"Last night at home," Rod sadly remarked. "They are coming to move me out in the morning."

"Don't give up yet, we will think of something," said Sam as she handed a cup filled with a multi-coloured mixture of pills to Rod, followed by a glass of water. "Night, Uncle Rod," said Sam. Pulling the door closed, she headed to the lounge to begin a clear-up operation before the council officials arrived in the morning.

Just as Sam began to tidy up, she heard sweet music drifting from the beach below. Walking out onto the cliff top, she saw a group of teenagers sitting around a fire on the beach. A boy was playing a guitar and the others were singing along. Sam recognised the tune as one of her favourites and she marvelled at the guitarist's marvellous melodies which were floating on the evening breeze. Unfortunately, she was tone deaf and possessed absolutely no musical skills, which further increased her admiration of the boy's musical performance.

Suddenly, the burning sensation returned in Sam's wrist, causing her to grab at the bangle and pull it from her wrist. Holding it up, she noticed it glowing in the fading light. Walking down the path to the beach, she noticed the bangle's glow had now faded.

Seeing Sam approaching, the guitarist stood up and turned to face her. "Hey, I'm Marcus," he said, offering a tattoo-covered hand in a show of friendship.

Reaching out her hand, Sam took hold of Marcus's hand, half anticipating what would happen next. All of a sudden, the boy jumped back as a loud crack of static jolted them apart.

"Crikey, are you supercharged?" he laughed, as Sam began to apologise. "Let's see if you can shock us with your guitar skills rather than electrocuting me," he said, offering the instrument to Sam. "Come on, give us a tune."

Taking the guitar, Sam began to strum away and was

amazed at the results. Rather than the tuneless sounds she had been reprimanded for producing during music lessons at school, she created a tuneful song which filled the night air. Sam didn't know how she was doing it, but she played a note-perfect version of the song which Marcus had performed only minutes earlier. After a rousing round of applause, Sam began to strum away again, playing another familiar tune she had heard on the radio only days earlier. Again, it was note-perfect!

After handing the guitar back to Marcus, she headed back to the beach house. Sam considered what had just happened. Her mind cogs ticked and whirred as she processed the events of the day. Since she had put on this mysterious golden bangle, she seemed to have gained the ability to carry out new skills which she had previously been unable to perform.

Everything fitted into place. She was draining the skills from the people she watched, and the electrical surge during the handshake seemed to be the moment the ability transferred across to her body. It sounded totally ridiculous, but it had to be true as it had happened twice in the space of a few hours. As sleep began to take over Sam's world, an idea crept into her head.

The morning came far too quickly and Sam awoke, still half asleep and feeling little refreshment after her late night. Moving through to Uncle Rod's bedroom, Sam helped the old man to his feet before helping him wash and dress.

Leaving Uncle Rod sitting wearily on his bed, Sam

looked through the window to see a car making its way up the dusty track towards the beach house. She watched as the vehicle got closer, dust billowing up from the tyres as it bounced along the track.

Dashing back into the bedroom, Sam slipped the bangle from her wrist and pushed it onto Rod's frail arm. The old man looked at her with a confused expression. Sam stepped back and began to briskly walk back and forth across the worn carpet as Rod watched on. She began to frantically bounce from foot to foot while waving her arms in the air, before lying face down and completing a set of press-ups. The old man watched in a shocked, speechless state of confusion. Sam's attention was drawn to the bangle as it began to glow red, making Rod jerk his arm up in the air and yelp out with a mixture of shock and surprise.

"Right, we're good to go," said Sam with a grin. Throwing her arms around Rod, she hugged the old man tightly. Both of their bodies shook and wobbled as a powerful electrical surge made its way from Sam into Rod. Pulling away and giving a further confused shake of his head, Rod rubbed at the skin around the bangle. "Whatever you do, don't take it off," instructed Sam.

She disappeared through the door and Rod leaned over and watched Sam cross the lounge and open the front door, to be faced by two men in sharp suits.

"We're here to collect Rod Grimes," said one of the men bluntly. "We have instructions to take him to the Tall Trees Nursing Home. The doctor says he isn't well enough to live on his own any more as he can't get about. Have you packed him a bag?"

The other man simply stood with his arms folded and chewed on a piece of gum. Both men wore expressions which signalled that they meant business. Sam opened her mouth and began to speak, when without warning, Rod's voice boomed out from the bedroom.

"I don't think I will be coming with you chaps today," explained Rod as he energetically bounded out into the lounge with a huge grin on his face. The men's facial expressions changed instantly. Beginning to leap from foot to foot, Uncle Rod performed a breath-taking workout routine which shocked the men into a stunned silence. Their mouths hung open as they watched the old man star jump up and down like an energetic child in a PE lesson. Next, he dropped to the floor and performed a set of press-ups. Whereas before the old man had barely been able to walk and was unable to get very far, he now effortlessly lifted his body up and down, time after time. Standing up and brushing his hands together, he looked at the men and smiled.

"Well, I must admit you do look in excellent shape, Mr Grimes," said the gum-chewing man, shaking his head in disbelief and looking blankly at the papers in his hand. "Sorry, it looks like there has been some kind of mistake. In fact, you look fitter than me, if I'm totally honest."

"Sorry for troubling you, Mr Grimes," apologised the other man, as they both made their way back to the car, still shaking their heads in utter astonishment at what they had witnessed.

Closing the door, Sam turned to Uncle Rod and smiled. The old man shook his head and grinned. "I don't know what happened there, but I don't care! We did it, Sam," he cried out before hugging Sam and crying tears of delight.

After explaining the story from the start, Sam stood and looked Uncle Rod in the eye. The old man reached down and began to take the golden bangle from his wrist, but Sam stopped him before he could remove it. "Keep it on. I have a feeling it'll make your life a lot easier. In fact, I reckon you'll be exactly the same as everyone else from now on," Sam said with a wink.

EGG-SPLORER

The classroom was silent, apart from a lone fly which zigzagged its way through the hot, sticky air. Pupils were slumped in their chairs forcing their eyes open as our teacher, Mr Royce, began to drone on once again. His voice temporarily drowned out the buzzing fly as it bounced from one window pane to another, seeking escape in a way we could only dream about.

"Atkins! Atkins!" bellowed Mr Royce, jolting me back to life and causing me to sit bolt upright in my seat. The whole class seemed to zone in on me and it felt like all their eyes were burning into me.

"Yes? Sorry, Sir. What were you saying, Sir?" I replied in a confused fashion which barely disguised the fact that I had been half asleep and totally unaware of anything which had taken place in the past half hour.

"Wake up lad!" he roared as he moved nearer, dragging his huge frame across the room towards me. "I'm waiting for an answer. Describe in detail the eggs of the Tyrannosaurus rex. This was your homework project and you have had over a week to complete it."

He stared at me, failing to break his icy gaze even for a split-second. This man was a machine! I moved my eyes away from him and searched around the room, seeking some sort of assistance or reassurance, but all I saw were faces which looked away and at anything apart from me. I was on my own and I had to find an answer, or at least an excuse to try and calm the situation.

You see, I'm not a lazy or idle person. Being a kid is tough. It means that I have such a hectic schedule that fitting everything in is a challenge at the best of times. Football, computer gaming, sleeping, eating - my life is busy, busy, busy from dawn till dusk! Plus, homework and learning are not high on my priority list and the worst bit is that Mr Royce knew this, which is why he picked me out. We were in November and he was still waiting for my first piece of homework this year.

"Err...it slipped my mind," I weakly replied, sinking in my seat to prepare for the volcanic eruption which would undoubtedly follow. The class started to shrink in their seats too, as if they knew what was coming next.

The reaction, as always, began in his large, round face, with a red glow which grew across his cheeks and tiny veins which began to bulge and pulse on his forehead. Mr Royce's hands began to tremble and shake and he opened his mouth, ready to unleash the fury which was growing inside him.

"Slipped your mind?" he viciously roared at a volume which literally pushed me back into my chair. "Get out of this classroom and take five minutes on the corridor to see if it slips back into your mind." Waving frantically towards the door, he visibly shook from head to toe with anger.

As I pushed my chair back, the grating sound on the floor echoed around the deathly silent room. Even the fly had thought it best to take cover and the buzzing had disappeared. Exiting through the door, I could hear Mr

Royce begin to talk again and the anger was still clear in his voice, until the door was pulled firmly shut and I leaned against the corridor wall.

Just as my shoulders began to relax and my body calmed, the classroom door swung open on its hinges and Mr Royce appeared like a rhino on the rampage. This was unexpected and I was not prepared for round two. He was holding his register and wearing a wicked grin across his chubby face.

"Do you realise this is the tenth piece of homework you have failed to complete?" he asked, knowing full well that I did. "Looks like I will need to bring your parents in."

"Well, I have done it," I replied, lying through my teeth and desperately trying to avoid any parental involvement which could lead to groundings and serious loss of football and gaming time. Tapping my head with one outstretched finger, I explained, "It's all up here, you see, nothing written down."

"Ah, is that right?" he replied as he nodded away. "Well you better get those ideas in that head of yours sorted out as you are first up to present to the class. We can't wait to hear all your dinosaur egg facts. Otherwise, I will be making that call home." Turning on the heels of his polished, black shoes, he disappeared into the classroom and slammed the door behind him.

I was in a real pickle! I had successfully managed to wriggle my way out of many problems during my time at school, but this had taken things to a new level and provided me with a new and challenging dilemma. As I saw it I had two options. I could own up, which would mean I would most certainly be in lots of trouble, or I could stand up and make up some nonsense facts about dinosaurs and dinosaur eggs. Neither sounded like a winning solution and, according to the clock, I was running out of time and the chances of my parents finding out were increasing by the second.

As I stood pondering my no-win situation, Mr Clark, the caretaker, appeared down the corridor carrying his mop and bucket. As he got nearer, he smiled and nodded at me. He knew I wasn't a bad sort, but to be fair he would have seen me standing on the corridor a few times as my class was opposite his office. In fact, Mr Clark was probably the staff member who I treated with the greatest respect. That was for one reason; his stories. Mr Clark was a master storyteller who spun the most incredible tales about adventures in far-off lands and amazing places, many of which were told while I was standing on the corridor or waiting outside the Headteacher's office. To be honest, his skills were wasted mopping out toilets and mending broken shelves.

Unlocking the door to his office, he disappeared inside, only to return shortly after and shuffle off down the corridor, leaving the door to his office ajar. The corridor was deserted once again and I felt like a lonely figure on the outside of everyone else's world.

Suddenly, my eyes were drawn to the open door. Now I didn't do this on purpose, but it just simply happened. I walked over to the open door, double checking the coast was clear before pushing it open. Curiosity had got the better of me and I walked in, to be hit by the smell of detergent and cleaning products. The shelves were littered with various tools and cans. There was a broken washbasin in one corner of the room and a desk piled high with junk was pushed up against the wall next to the window.

Shafts of light shone through the filthy panes and highlighted an old, rusty object on the shelf. I made my way over and lifted it from the shelf. It was an old oil can, the type with a long nozzle and a pump-action handle. It looked ancient and was layered with rust and grime. Holding the can in the air, I began to press the handle and at first it wouldn't budge as it was rusted in place. With more effort, it started to lower and rise, fortunately with no oil spurting from the nozzle.

What happened next is totally incredible. My arms began to rise up and the can was lifted into the air. Now that may seem normal until I tell you I was not in control of my arms and what was happening! Once the can was level with my forehead, my thumb began to repeatedly pump the handle. I tried to stop. I tried to drop the can. I could do neither! My thumb was now raising and lowering the handle at such speed that it was nothing but a blur. I was being pulled by an invisible force into the oil can. Dizziness began to swamp me and the room began to spin. Everything went black and the curtains were closed on my world.

As I half-opened my eyes, I looked through eyelash

blinds in an attempt to work out what had happened. Endless lines of trees surrounded me like soldiers standing to attention. The trees were like skyscrapers and towered high into the clear, blue sky.

Fully opening my eyes, I began to sit myself up from the position I had found myself in. My hands were wet and the grass underneath me was soaking. The air was sticky and humid. One thing was for sure though, I definitely was no longer in school. I was in some sort of forest or jungle, judging by the dense undergrowth and huge trees. But how could this be? Looking down on the floor beside me was the answer - the oil can.

Sweat trickled down my neck and under my shirt collar as I stood up. It was boiling hot and the heat seemed to attack me from all angles. Looking up through the tree canopy, I saw birds gliding across the backdrop of the blue sky. Scrunching up my eyes, I looked hard and a wave of fear and dread surged through my body. Those 'birds' were like nothing I had seen before and didn't resemble anything like the seagulls which I was used to seeing at home. They were huge, and had wings ten times the size of the birds I was familiar with. Their beaks were long and pointed and their huge feet had long talons curving from them. These were no seagulls. They were pterodactyls! These creatures had been supposedly wiped out millions of years ago, but I was looking at them with my own eyes!

My mind raced and fear began to take over. I needed to get home and the sooner the better. Picking up the oil can, I was about to push the lever when something happened which froze me like a statue. The ground began to shake beneath my feet. The vibrations were travelling through my body and I looked between the trees in all directions to find out what was causing the shock waves.

Heart thumping out of my chest and fear clenching my throat like an invisible hand, I scurried through the trees, dodging and dashing until I reached a large rock pile. I pushed my body close to the stack and tried to calm my breathing, which was now ragged and out of control. The thumping noise became stronger and louder and whatever was causing it was getting closer. My chest felt like it would explode. Then it happened. The moment which will be burned into my memory forever!

The never-ending screen of trees began to shake and wobble, causing loose leaves to flutter down to the jungle floor. The sound of breaking branches and rustling leaves was clear to hear. My eyes were fixed hard on the direction the noise was coming from and I fought the adrenaline which was surging around my body and telling me to run for my life.

Suddenly, the trees before me began to part like a pair of curtains being opened in the morning and I was confronted with the most terrifying sight. Two orange eyes blazed in my direction and were accompanied by a colossal set of jaws, which gaped open revealing a set of gigantic teeth, each one bigger than my entire body. Two huge nostrils flared open as the beast raised its head and released a deafening roar which caused me to shield my ears and let me know that I was in the domain of the king of the dinosaurs, the Tyrannosaurus rex. The beast towered high above the tree tops and its gargantuan body simply brushed the trees aside as if they were saplings. The creature's tail moved from side to side in a snake-like movement which swept debris one way then the other.

Trying to control the feeling of panic which was flooding my limbs, I reached into my pocket and pulled out my camera phone. Raising the camera above the rocks, but taking care not to be spotted, I tried in vain to capture the beast's image as it stepped into full view. As my thumb pressed on the screen, my heart temporarily froze. The clicking noise echoed around the forest, causing the beast to swing its head towards me and raise its nose in the air as it sniffed and searched for my scent.

Pushing myself against the rocks, I held my breath and prayed. The ground shook violently, which signalled it was on the move again. Peering over the boulders, I could see he was heading in my direction, but something else caught my eye. The rocks I was hiding behind formed part of a stone circle, and in the middle of them were smooth, brown, egg-shaped rocks. Then it dawned on me. They were dinosaur eggs, and my hiding place was a dinosaur nest!

The creature was still lumbering its way towards the nest and I could no longer see the trees behind it as its massive body eclipsed them. Again, the beast opened its jaws and roared a violent warning, which made my ears ring and my head shake. Still it continued its unrelenting march towards me and the nest.

Picking up the oil can and half crawling and half rolling, I made a break for it. An old tree stood a few metres from my hiding place and I could see it had a hollowed out section in the trunk, just large enough for me to squeeze into. Inserting my body into the opening, I moulded myself to the space and stayed as still as my trembling body would allow.

Without warning, the tree began to shake violently and horrendous creaking and groaning noises rang out around my hiding space. Looking through a small opening in the tree trunk, I could see the creature battering and pounding at the tree in an attempt to get access to its prey!

Bark showered down onto me, filling my mouth and causing me to spit out chunks of wood. I could feel the tree beginning to lean and knew it wouldn't be long before the monster used its powerful claws to drag me out and devour me.

In one last, hopeful attempt, I began to squeeze the handle of the oil can and it moved downwards. Making use of the adrenaline which coursed through me, I pumped at the handle repeatedly, just as the tree creaked and toppled over. Closing my eyes, I prepared myself for the end.

As I slowly opened my eyes, I looked around and gave a sigh of relief. Rather than trees and bushes, I was surrounded by paint cans, tools and piles of assorted junk. I was safe at last and back in Mr Clark's office. Regaining my feet and moving towards the door, I walked back onto the deserted corridor and pulled the door closed behind me.

Seconds after I had emerged from the room, the classroom door burst open and the gigantic frame of Mr Royce lumbered out in a similar way to the dinosaur I'd encountered only minutes before. He looked me up and down and stared inquisitively at the oil can which I was still clutching in my right hand.

"Right then, Atkins," he cruelly hissed. "I think it's time for your little homework presentation and you can explain about this oil can later." Snatching the object from my grasp, he ushered me back into the sweat-drenched, boredom-filled atmosphere of the classroom. Leaving me standing alone at the front of the class, he hobbled off and plonked himself down at the back of the class. "Off you go, lad. This should be really interesting!" he said in a mocking tone.

The atmosphere in the room could have been cut with a knife. The class generally felt sorry for me, I think, but most of them were also grateful it was me and not them who was up there facing the humiliation they were about to witness.

Calmly, I reached into my pocket, took out my phone and connected it to a long, black cable which was attached to the computer screen. Switching on my phone, I selected my photograph file which caused an image to ping up on the screen for all to see. The class gasped and whispers broke out like wildfire. Mr Royce raised the small, circular glasses from around his neck and perched them on his nose.

There on the wall was a crystal-clear image of the gigantic beast I had been face to face with a short while earlier. Every terrifying detail was there for all to see. But it got better, as in the foreground of the picture were the dinosaur eggs. As I started to speak and talk through what had happened, right from the oil can to the T-rex, the class stared in astonished silence and hung on my every word until I finished, at which point they all stood up and applauded loudly.

"Silence! Silence! I have never heard such nonsense!" bellowed Mr Royce. The class fell silent on his command and all eyes shifted to him as he moved towards me. "I have never heard such a pack of lies in my life. I'll give you one thing, you can make up a story! I think I'll share that with your parents when I phone them tonight. You expect me to believe that an oil can transported you back to the Jurassic times? Do you think I am a complete idiot?"

Well needless to say, after the day I had gone through and the amount of bother I was in, I thought it best not to answer that question. Instead, I stood in silence and watched Mr Royce lift the oil can up as he closely inspected it. I watched as he began to pump the handle repeatedly. I also watched the horrified look on his face seconds before he disappeared into the can before our eyes!

After I had given my side of the events to the Head, I was allowed home while the search for Mr Royce continued. I awaited the dreaded phone call that night which would seal my fate and land me in hot water with my parents. But it never came.

That was the first of a series of strange events. The next day we were all called to an emergency assembly. The Head explained to the school the circumstances surrounding the mysterious disappearance of Mr Royce. Turns out he was never seen again, neither him nor the old oil can.

Finally we come to Mr Clark, who was the original owner of the oil can. The saddest result of the whole episode was that during the rest of my days at school he never told me any more stories about incredible adventures and long forgotten places. It was almost as if he had run out of ideas!

ACKNOWLEDGEMENTS

Thank you to Mum and Dad for their love, unwavering support and guidance throughout the years. I know in my heart that Mum will be reading this book from afar.

Extra special thanks must go to Susan O'Malley, Jackie Simpson, Judy Earnshaw, Lesley Bennett, Sandra Mangan and Phil and Annette Whiteley for their hard work, constructive feedback and valued advice during the editing and proofing process.

Jason Bottomley's ICT skills were invaluable when I eventually got to the front cover design stage. His technological know-how helped me massively to bring together my vision.

I would like to extend my appreciation to Hayley Oakes, who shared her experiences of self-publishing with me, making the unknown journey much clearer.

Many other people have been there for me along the way with supportive words, encouragement and help with the promotion and publicity of 'Impossible Tales!' This input has been extremely helpful and will be forever valued.

A NOTE FROM THE AUTHOR

Firstly, I would like to thank you so much for reading 'Impossible Tales!' and I sincerely hope that you enjoyed the stories as much as I loved writing them. Fingers crossed it might inspire you to put pen to paper and create a story and who knows, one day, a book of your own!

I started out as a Primary teacher in my hometown of Blackpool, Lancashire in 1998, before changing career after fifteen fantastic years working with hundreds of brilliant children.

Writing stories for children has always been my dream and 'Impossible Tales!' is my first published book. These stories have rattled around inside my head for many years, so it is a wonderful feeling to finally share them.

When I'm not writing, I work as a professional storyteller and visit different venues, where I spin all manner of yarns and tales for children, which cover a wide variety of topics and themes.

Made in the USA
Columbia, SC
05 October 2017